'You will come and stay with me.'

His eyes met hers across the table. It was at that point that Natalie wondered if, for the very first time, Adam was seeing her as a woman and not as the kid sister of his old friend, or even as a professional colleague. The thought threw her into mild, temporary confusion.

Dear Reader

Can you put the past behind you? Jenny Ashe poses this question in THE CALL OF LOVE, while Sarah Franklin looks at obsessive behaviour in THE WESSEX SUMMER. No claims for a cure, but sometimes help can be found. In WAITING GAME, Laura MacDonald explores the passage from infatuation to love, in a touching story, while Judith Worthy gives us a heroine who married the wrong brother—the right one is *very* right. . . Australian Cam Walters is every woman's dream!

See you next month!

The Editor

Laura MacDonald lives in the Isle of Wight. She is married and has a grown-up family. She has enjoyed writing fiction since she was a child, but for several years she has worked for members of the medical profession both in pharmacy and in general practice. Her daughter is a nurse and has helped with the research for Laura's Medical Romances.

Recent titles by the same author:

LOVE CHANGES EVERYTHING
ALWAYS ON MY MIND

WAITING GAME

BY

LAURA MacDONALD

MILLS & BOON LIMITED
ETON HOUSE   18–24 PARADISE ROAD
RICHMOND   SURREY   TW9 1SR

*First published in Great Britain 1992
by Mills & Boon Limited*

© Laura MacDonald 1992

*Australian copyright 1992
Philippine copyright 1992
This edition 1992*

ISBN 0 263 77780 4

*Set in 10½ on 12½ pt Linotron Times
03-9207-46206*

*Typeset in Great Britain by Centracet, Cambridge
Made and printed in Great Britain*

CHAPTER ONE

A SKIRL of bagpipes heralded the toast-master, but for a moment Natalie Fraser allowed her gaze to wander from her brother James and his new bride to a tall, broad-shouldered man on the far side of the banqueting hall.

She had thought he wouldn't come to the wedding, and she hadn't in fact realised he was there until after the service when the bride and groom were posing for photographs.

Her heart had leapt at her first glimpse of him, but he had merely given her a polite nod of recognition before getting into his car, and it was not until now at the wedding breakfast that she'd had the chance to study him.

It had been three years since she'd last seen Adam Curtis, and she was curious to see if the traumatic events of those years had changed him.

He had always been a powerfully built man, muscular without an ounce of spare flesh, and in that respect he seemed the same, but while his hair was still thick and dark there were traces of grey at the temples that certainly hadn't been there in the days when she'd had a schoolgirl crush on him.

'Ladies and gentlemen, the bride and groom!' The toast-master called for the assembled company to raise their glasses, and Natalie forced herself to concentrate.

Her new sister-in-law looked radiant in a gown of ivory satin, her dark hair covered by a Juliet cap with an attached veil edged with seed-pearls. As Kirsty smiled up into her husband's face Natalie felt a pang as she wondered if she would ever stand before the altar in their local kirk and celebrate afterwards at a wedding breakfast at Craigie Court.

She was pleased, however, that her brother seemed to have found happiness at last, and nothing on earth would have persuaded her to deny James that moment. There were twelve years between herself and James, and as he had reached his late thirties Natalie had found herself wondering if he would ever settle down and marry.

As James stood up to reply to the toast Natalie remembered that Adam Curtis was of a similar age, as he and James had been at medical school together. Casually she stole another glance in his direction, her curiosity once again getting the better of her.

He was leaning against one of the ornamental pillars that formed two columns down the centre of the banqueting hall. His expression was inscrutable and he appeared to be listening intently to what James was saying. She was about to look away when she noticed him draw his brows together in a deep frown, almost as if he was hiding some inner tension, and she wondered what he of all people must be thinking today.

Natalie had first met Adam Curtis when he and James had been housemen at the same Midlands hospital, and James had on several occasions brought him home to Pitlochry

She had been at school at the time and had developed an instant crush on the handsome doctor. He had been kind to her in a remote sort of way, while she had hung on his every word, reading some meaning into every glance, grateful for any scrap of attention, however small.

This had continued until one Christmas after Adam had become a registrar and James a GP. James had met up with Adam quite by chance and invited him home to Pitlochry. Natalie had been ecstatic, as she had been wondering if she would ever see Adam again after the two men had embarked on their seperate careers.

But her joy was to be short-lived, for that particular Christmas the Fraser household had another guest, James's and Natalie's cousin, Suzanne Drummond.

From the moment Adam had seen Suzanne he hardly seemed to notice Natalie's existence, for he had eyes for no one else.

Not that he would have noticed her anyway, thought Natalie ruefully as she watched James and Kirsty cut their wedding cake; she's been an awkward teenager at the time, painfully thin and with her red hair in a most unbecoming style, while Suzanne—well, Suzanne had been a fashion model for a top London agency, and exquisitely beautiful.

Natalie could clearly remember agonising at just how gorgeous Suzanne looked, with her wild tousled mane of golden hair, her green slanting eyes and her long legs that seemed to go on forever.

She recalled ruefully how she had spent hours in her room in front of the mirror trying to do something with her thick, straight red hair and to get rid of the smattering of freckles across her nose and cheeks—in fact, anything to make Adam Curtis notice her instead of Suzanne.

It had all been in vain of course; he had barely acknowledged her and oh, how it had hurt. She gave a grim little smile at the memory.

Suddenly she felt she needed some air and, glancing round the huge elegant room, she saw that the french windows on the far side were open.

Still clutching her glass of champagne, she threaded her way through the round tables, each one covered with a cream lace cloth and decorated with deep pink flowers and ribbons to match the dresses of the two young bridesmaids. Pausing a few times among the assembled guests, she returned greetings and spoke briefly to one or two elderly relatives, some of whom she hadn't seen for several years.

Just before she stepped on to the terrace she glanced back at the top table and caught a glimpse of her father's face. He looked proud and happy, and she smiled, then felt a momentary pang as she wished her mother could have lived to see James marry Kirsty McLeod, the daughter of her best friend.

The wedding breakfast was taking place at Craigie Court, a sprawling eighteenth-century mansion built in grey stone and famous for its breathtaking views of Loch Tummel, which had once been so beloved by Queen Victoria.

Natalie took a deep breath and leaned on the stone parapet. It was one of those glorious autumn days when the rich copper of the beech trees and the deep green pines looked unreal against a cobalt-blue sky.

'Mind if I join you?'

The voice was deep and instantly recognisable, and Natalie felt herself stiffen. 'Of course not,' she said, only half turning.

'I find weddings claustrophobic.'

'Yes,' she replied, understanding.

Then, surprisingly, he smiled. It was a tight smile and didn't reach his dark eyes, but it was a smile nevertheless. 'I find it difficult to cope with people's false sense of importance.'

She laughed. 'I know exactly what you mean.'

As she spoke she glanced back through the french doors, where the resonant tones of a certain female relative could quite clearly be heard as she ordered some of the guests to pose for a family photograph.

'So how are you, Natalie?' He too leaned on the parapet beside her, but after briefly surveying the view he turned his head and she was aware of his close scrutiny.

'I'm well, Adam; and you? James tells me you're flying high these days.'

He gave a slight grimace as if dismissing any accolade, but Natalie knew he now stood at the very peak of his career. Her brother had chosen the field of general practice, taking over the Pitlochry practice from their father on his recent retirement, but Adam Curtis had elected to go into surgery and was now a consultant surgeon in a top London hospital.

They were silent for a moment, then Adam turned and leaned back on the stonework so that he could study her even more closely. 'Forthcoming nuptials must make people more talkative—James has also been telling me about you.'

Natalie looked startled. 'That sounds ominous. Whatever has he been saying?'

'Simply that you've done very well in your career. Theatre sister, isn't it?'

She nodded, unable to prevent a sudden rush of pride.

'Here in Pitlochry?'

'Yes.'

'Do you enjoy it?'

'Oh, yes, more than anything,' she replied fervently.

Something in her manner must have intrigued him, for, straightening up, he indicated the steps down to the lawns below. 'Shall we take a walk? That is, if you don't think anyone will miss us.'

'I shouldn't think they would—they're all far too busy being important.' She turned and fell into step beside him, a light breeze tugging at the full skirt of her dress. The dress had cost her a fortune, but as soon as she had set eyes on it she knew she had to have it, for the shade of aquamarine provided a perfect foil for her Titian hair and clear grey eyes.

Slowly they descended the steps, silently admiring the vastness and splendour of the view as they went. Then as they reached the lawns and the sight of the loch slipped away behind the belt of trees he said, 'You were saying how much you enjoy your work.'

'Yes, it's my life.'

'Your whole life?' His dark eyebrows rose questioningly. 'You mean there isn't any likelihood of another peal of wedding bells in the Fraser household in the immediate future?'

She gave a short laugh. 'Oh, no, nothing like that. I'm too involved with my work.' It was an excuse and she knew it, but for some reason she didn't want Adam probing too deeply into her personal life. How could she ever have explained that the few relationships she'd had all seemed to fizzle out before they became too serious and that her secret fantasy had always been that one day she would meet him again?

'Have you ever thought of working in London?'

The question was casual, but Natalie thought she detected an edge to his voice. She shook her head. 'No, I've always been quite happy here.'

He didn't pursue the matter further, and they carried on in silence, walking across the short emerald grass until they reached the belt of pines that bordered the loch.

As the sparkling water came into sight again they paused, and Natalie wondered if she should mention Suzanne, but before she had the chance Adam said, 'You know, you really are lucky, living here—that surely must be one of the most magnificent views of all time.'

She nodded. 'Another reason why I've had no desire to leave.'

He smiled, and she was struck by the fine lines around his eyes. 'I can understand that. I too enjoy my brief visits to Scotland.'

'It's been a long time since we've seen you, Adam.' She said it softly, and for a moment he turned his face away as if he was studying the view afresh, but not before she had noticed the frown that crossed his forehead again. 'I . . . I was so sorry about Suzanne,' she went on hesitantly, aware that anything she said would sound inadequate but at the same time knowing it had to be said.

He gave a faint shrug just as the breeze caught his dark hair, lifting it away from his face and giving him a boyish, slightly vulnerable look. 'Thank you.' He gave a brief nod, then, abruptly changing the subject, he said, 'I'm glad James and Kirsty finally named the day. I was beginning to think they'd never get around to it.'

'Didn't we all?' she smiled.

'I understand James is taking over from your father.'

She nodded. 'Yes, I think it's always been understood that one day he would, and now seems the
obvious time.'

'So where does that leave you?'

'Me?' She looked puzzled.

'You still live at home, don't you?'

'Oh, yes. But it's a large house and my father will
continue to live there.'

Adam declined to answer, and Natalie knew
instinctively that he was thinking that that particular
arrangement wouldn't work now that James was
bringing a wife home. It was something that had
occurred to her and had bothered her frequently
ever since James had named his wedding date, but
she didn't intend letting Adam Curtis know that.

She suddenly shivered as the breeze became even
more playful, whipping tendrils of her hair across
her face. In silent mutual agreement they turned
away from the loch and began to make their way
back across the carpet of pine needles to the hotel
lawns.

When they had almost reached the steps James
suddenly appeared on the terrace and leaned over
the parapet.

'Oh, there you are,' he called. 'I wondered where
you'd got to. Kirsty's gone to change; we'll be
leaving shortly.'

They were climbing the steps to the terrace when
Adam suddenly said, 'If you ever change your mind
about working in London, let me know.'

She turned curiously. 'Are you serious?'

'Very. My theatre sister is leaving in a few months' time to have a baby—damned inconsiderate of her.'

Suddenly Natalie was aware that her heart had begun to beat very fast and she seemed totally incapable of giving him an intelligent answer.

He shrugged again. 'Think it over,' he said abruptly. 'Now, if you'll excuse me, I'll go and have a few words with your father.' By this time they had reached the terrace, and with a friendly nod to James he disappeared through the french windows, leaving Natalie staring after him.

'What's up, Nat? You look puzzled. What's Adam been saying to you.' James grinned down at her as she reached his side. He looked handsome in his Highland dress, the rich tartan, the velvet jacket and crisp frilled shirt against his deep auburn hair and beard, and she felt a sudden rush of affection for him.

She gave herself a little shake. 'Oh, nothing much—I was surprised to see him here, that's all. I knew he'd had an invitation, but in the circumstances I thought he might refuse.'

James nodded. 'I must admit, I thought the same, but I'm glad he did come. Adam and I go back a long way.' He smiled as if remembering their days as junior housemen.

'Does he ever mention Suzanne?' asked Natalie, lowering her voice as a group of guests suddenly appeared on the terrace.

James's smile disappeared. 'No, never, not today

nor on any of the other occasions I've seen him in the past three years. In fact, I sometimes wonder if he's ever got over her death or whether he's just shut it from his mind. Today must have brought back so many memories of his own wedding, especially here at Craigie Court.' He paused and they both turned and looked back at the loch, then he added quietly, 'He worshipped her, you know.'

Natalie nodded. 'Yes, I know.' They fell silent, each recalling the day when Adam Curtis had married their cousin Suzanne.

It had been high summer, the loch had been as blue as the sky above, the grounds of Craigie Court swathed in a mantle of green, and there had been roses everywhere. Red roses and white roses; decorating the pillars in the banqueting hall, clustered at the ends of the pews in the kirk, entwined in the bridesmaids' hair and cascading to the ground from Suzanne's bouquet. To this very day Natalie could not see red or white roses without being reminded of the day when her cousin had married Adam Curtis.

She herself had been a bridesmaid, one of six attendants; a matron of honour—a friend of Suzanne's from the fashion world and nearly as glamorous—two tiny pageboys and a flower girl, and herself and another cousin, all in cream wild silk.

And Suzanne, looking as if she'd stepped straight from the pages of a book of fairy stories with her mane of hair, the colour of ripe wheat, tumbling over her shoulders, and her perfect figure, which had looked as if it had been poured into her dress of ivory raw silk.

Suzanne had insisted that Adam wore the Highland dress of her family clan, which he had done without protest. But Natalie had suspected that he would have done anything to please her, for, as James had just reminded her, he had indeed worshipped Suzanne.

And throughout it all Natalie had smiled, burying her own girlish dreams so that no one would guess what she'd suffered as she'd watched her secret love marry another.

It had been a golden day, full of beauty, love, laughter and sunshine, in cruel, stark contrast to another day less than three years later when the families gathered again, this time for a very different reason.

And, just as before, the weather had fitted the occasion, with a thick mist that had enveloped the valley, the kirk, and the bleak graveyard where Adam Curtis had laid his wife to rest.

The accident had been quite horrific, the details haunting Natalie to the present day. Suzanne had been driving her E-type Jaguar on the M1 very late at night, when the car had gone out of control, hit the central reservation and collided with an articulated lorry before bursting into flames.

Her body, when it was finally pulled from the wrecked car, had been totally unrecognisable as that of the beautiful fashion model whose face was known to millions.

At the funeral and the small family gathering afterwards at the Drummond home Natalie could hardly bring herself to look at Adam's gaunt face, his grief and suffering etched into every line. After his marriage she had done her utmost to put him out of her mind and had gone out with other men, although none of the relationships had ever really become serious.

When Suzanne was killed, after the initial shock and horror it had occurred to Natalie that Adam was free again, although she had hated herself at the time for even contemplating what she would like to happen. But then when the months passed and he didn't visit Pitlochry again and there was not so much as a word from him she had almost been forced to accept that he had gone out of her life forever—until today.

She glanced at James and, knowing him as she did, she knew his thoughts also had progressed from Adam's wedding-day to the tragic events that had followed.

'It was brave of him to come,' she said, then casually she asked, 'Has there been anyone else in his life since Suzanne?'

James shook his head. 'I don't know, but I wouldn't have thought so.'

'She would certainly be a hard act to follow,' agreed Natalie, 'but it would be nice to think he could find someone else.'

'Didn't you have a crush on him once?' James smiled suddenly.

'Yes, and that's all it was,' she lied, 'a schoolgirl
crush. He didn't even know I existed.' She gave a
short laugh. 'And let's face it, he wouldn't with
Suzanne around, would he?'

James laughed. 'She was pretty stunning, wasn't
she? But that was all a long time ago. It would be a
different story now.'

'Whatever do you mean?' She stared at James.

'You were a child then, Nat. Have you looked in
the mirror lately? Old Adam couldn't have failed to
notice the difference.'

She flushed at this rare praise from her brother,
who was not usually given to displays of appreci-
ation. 'Don't be silly,' she said stiffly, then, glancing
up, was glad to see that Kirsty was back in the hall
after changing out of her wedding dress. How could
she have even begun to explain to her brother the
secret dreams she had cherished for so long?
Dreams in which she and Adam Curtis met again?

It wasn't until much later, after James and Kirsty
had departed on their honeymoon to the Canary
Islands amid a cacophony of bagpipes and car horns,
the visiting relatives had dispersed to their homes,
and Natalie and her father had returned home to
the house in Pitlochry, that she had time to muse
over her brother's remark.

She made a pot of tea and carried it through to
the drawing-room, where she placed it on a low
table in front of the fire, then drew the curtains to
shut out the chill of the autumn night.

She thankfully sank down on to the sofa, and with

their two black Labradors at her feet she gave herself up to the luxury of thinking over the events of the day.

James had implied that Adam Curtis could well be attracted to her now, but she hardly dared even to contemplate that prospect, and, besides, if what James had said was true then Adam still hadn't got over Suzanne's death, so he'd hardly be likely to be interested in her.

But what James didn't know was that Adam had as good as offered her a job on his unit. She felt her pulses race at the thought, then she tried to dismiss it. Maybe he had only been making polite conversation and hadn't meant it.

No, she thought as she replaced her cup in its saucer and saw with a smile that her father, exhausted by the events of the day, had fallen asleep, Adam Curtis's interest in her had probably been purely professional, but he had asked her to think over his proposal.

Natalie knew that if anyone had asked her a week ago if she would even consider thinking of changing her job and moving to London she would have told them there was no chance.

But that would have been before Adam Curtis had walked back into her life, and Natalie had a feeling that now that had happened nothing would ever be quite the same again.

CHAPTER TWO

NATALIE rinsed her hands and arms and reflectively watched the lather swirl away. It was a Monday morning and there was a full list facing the operating team. The scrub nurse had already fastened the ties on the surgeon's mask before he scrubbed up, and he too now wiped his hands on sterile towels before dropping them in the disposal unit. He had studied the morning's list in her office when he had arrived and he knew the first patient was a middle-age lady whom he'd seen in Out-patients suffering from gall-bladder problems, and who had now been admitted for a cholecystectomy.

Natalie followed him as he walked from the scrub-room into the theatre, where the patient, fully anaesthetised, and the theatre team were ready and waiting for him.

'Good morning.' He nodded to the other members of the team—his assistant, Dr Uri Adahbi, the anaesthetist, Jon Bell, three members of the nursing staff and two orderlies.

'Good morning, Mr Curtis.' The murmured chorus was polite, respectful, but Adam Curtis was the type of man that easily commanded respect. He demanded high standards from his staff, but equally his staff seemed only too willing to reach and maintain those standards.

'If there are no problems, shall we get started?' He glanced around as he spoke and for the briefest of moments his eyes met Natalie's as she turned to supervise a student nurse who had come to watch the operation. They were a pair of expressive dark eyes above his mask, and for a moment they gazed steadily into hers.

Not for the first time Natalie found herself wondering at the events of the past few weeks, events that had resulted in her being in charge of Adam's theatre on this busy Monday morning. She'd been on his team now for just two weeks, but it was long enough to convince her that professionally at least she had made the right decision.

She glanced down at the patient; green sterile towels covered her abdomen, with just a rectangle of flesh exposed. Jon Bell was in position at the patient's head and the rest of the team were poised, ready for action.

After an enquiring look at Jon Bell, who nodded in response, Adam took the scalpel from the scrub nurse to make his incision. Dr Adahbi moved forward with the diathermy equipment to control the bleeding and the operation was under way.

Natalie motioned to the student to step forward, and they watched as Adam made his incision below the patient's right lower rib, deepening it through layers of fat, abdominal muscle and peritoneum. As he worked he carefully explained each procedure he carried out, his deep pleasant voice, slightly muffled behind his mask, echoing in the hollow atmosphere of the theatre.

After exploring the abdominal cavity he checked with the lighted X-ray plates that Natalie had prepared earlier, then, when he had satisfied himself that there were no further complications, he retracted the liver to gain access to the gall-bladder.

As the operation progressed Adam continued explaining each step, mainly for the benefit of the wide-eyed student, although Natalie noticed he had the attention of everyone else in the theatre. While he checked the bile duct for the presence of calculi Dr Adahbi passed a fine catheter into the cystic duct to prepare for the cholangiogram.

Once Adam was satisfied that all was progressing normally he removed the gall-bladder, opening it and taking out the stones.

'The patient will want these,' he explained to the student. 'She'll keep them in a jar by her bed and boast about them when her friends come to visit.'

His remark lightened the tension in the theatre, and as the operation progressed towards its conclusion Adam began talking to Jon Bell.

'How is Liz, Jon? I haven't seen her for some time.'

Jon shook his head. 'She's not too well at the moment, as it happens; fighting a bout of flu, actually.'

'I'm sorry to hear that.'

Natalie, glancing at the two men, guessed from

their conversation that Adam was quite friendly with the Bells.

'Yes, it's a shame. I had two tickets for *Les Misérables* tonight, but. . .' Jon shrugged, then, glancing up, he said quickly, 'I suppose you wouldn't like them, Adam? It'd be a pity if they went to waste.'

'I'd be pleased to go, thanks, Jon.' Adam glanced up from the table as he spoke and his eyes once again met Natalie's. 'Maybe Sister Fraser would like to accompany me?'

The tension in the theatre was suddenly heightened as the team waited to hear Natalie's reply.

For a moment she didn't know what to say, then she mumbled, 'Oh, I don't know, really. . .I. . .'

'Oh, come on, Sister,' Adam had allowed a note of amusement to creep into his tone now. 'Don't tell me you've seen *Les Mis*?'

'No. . .but. . .'

'Well, there you are, then; now's your chance.'

He turned away, then, as the staff moved forward to transfer the patient to the recovery-room, he paused as Uri Adahbi said, 'Have you met this new adminstrator yet, Mr Curtis?'

Adam frowned. 'Who do you mean?'

'His name's Roger Lomax, and I've got a feeling he's going to be trouble.'

'Oh, not another one.' Adam sighed as he peeled of his latex gloves and dropped them into the waste bag. 'The last one was bad enough.'

'Apparently this one's worse. According to the

orthopaedic registrar, he's incredibly tight over staff budgeting.'

'That's all we need,' remarked Adam, then, turning to Natalie again, he said, 'So what do you have next for us, Sister?'

'A seventy-five-year-old, Mr Thompson, for a transurethral prostatectomy in theatre three.'

'Ah, yes,' said Adam thoughtfully. 'I remember Mr Thompson, a wonderful old boy, a real character. Shall we get started, then, Sister, if you're ready?'

As she moved forward to organise the second operation of the day Natalie found herself remembering how Adam had contacted her a couple of months after the wedding. She had been at home when his call had come through and the moment he had spoken she had recognised his voice, then, with the pleasantries over, he had said, 'Have you thought over what I asked you?'

'I have,' she had replied without hesitation.

'And?' he had prompted.

'I should like to apply,' she had told him firmly.

'Good,' he'd said. 'I do like a woman who knows what she wants. Christine will be leaving in about three months' time, so I'll send you an application form.'

She'd filled in the form, then been asked to attend an interview in London. She hadn't thought she would see Adam, but he had been on the panel which had interviewed her. Afterwards she was told almost immediately that she had the job, and Adam took her to lunch to celebrate.

'Here's to my new theatre sister,' he said, raising his glass while Natalie was still recovering from the shock of actually getting the job.

'Have you thought about accommodation?' he asked smoothly.

'Not really, although I had wondered if I could stay in the nurses' home just until I can find somewhere of my own.'

'I won't hear of it.' His eyes met hers across the table. 'You will come and stay with me.'

It was at that point that Natalie wondered if, for the very first time, Adam was seeing her as a woman and not as the kid sister of his old friend, or even as a professional colleague. The thought threw her into mild, temporary confusion.

'Oh, really, there's no need,' she replied, trying to sound casual. 'I'll be perfectly all right in the home.'

'No doubt you would be.' His reply was smooth but decisive. 'But you are family, Natalie. You'll be my guest until such time as you have your own home—and if you're worrying about hospital gossip,' a glint of amusement came into his dark eyes, 'you needn't, because my housekeeper and her young son live with me at Sheridan House.'

'Oh, I wasn't worried about that.' She felt the colour rise to her cheeks and hated herself for it. 'It's just that I wouldn't want to put you to any trouble.'

'I assure you there's no danger of that.'

It was decided, and his tone invited no further argument, but in the three months she had to wait while she had worked out her own notice and before she took up her position Natalie was in an agony of apprehension.

She was, however, totally unprepared for the sheer style and elegance of Sheridan House. It was a town house, three storeys high, and situated in the middle of a Regency terrace in a quiet cul-de-sac in the very heart of the city.

She had driven down from Scotland and arrived late on a cold, bleak February afternoon, to be welcomed by Adam's housekeeper.

Jane Markham was a round-faced, pleasant woman in her thirties with straight brown hair cut with a fringe above a pair of large owlish glasses. She seemed delighted at the prospect of female company, and over a cup of tea she explained to Natalie that her young son lived with her in her flat at the rear of the house.

'How old is your son?' Natalie asked as she followed the housekeeper to her bedroom on the second floor.

'He's seven, but, don't worry, he's very quiet; I'm sure he won't bother you.'

'I'm sure he won't.' Natalie smiled. 'I'll look forward to meeting him. I like children.'

'Mr Curtis is still at the hospital,' Jane explained as she bustled around the elegant room, drawing the curtains and shutting out the damp evening. 'But he should be home shortly.'

As Natalie unpacked she found herself in a mounting state of anticipation at the thought of seeing Adam again, but when he arrived home his attitude was polite but casual. Natalie was still feeling rather embarrassed at the fact of staying at his home, and she implied as much that evening when she and Adam met for dinner.

'There's no need, believe me. Most of the time I'm hardly here—in fact, I'm off to Brussels soon to lecture at the university, so you mustn't think you'll be in the way.'

'That's very kind of you, Adam,' she replied firmly, 'but, if you don't mind, I think it might be a good idea not to mention the fact that I'm staying here at the hospital.'

He appeared slightly amused by her request, but he agreed, and for the following two weeks he certainly appeared to be as good as his word, for she hardly saw him at Sheridan House. She invariably left before him in the mornings to start her shift, and in the evenings more often than not he was either lecturing, or attending some dinner or funtion, and she dined alone.

As the days passed Natalie was slowly and reluctantly forced to come to the conclusion that Adam's interest in her had indeed been only professional.

But now, right out of the blue, had come his invitation to join him to see *Les Misérables*, and as she followed him to theatre three to begin the second operation of the day she felt a tingle of excitement.

'So what's all this about Adam Curtis asking you out tonight?' Staff Nurse Lyn Irving grinned at Natalie as they enjoyed a well-earned cup of tea in the staff canteen.

'My word, news certainly travels fast in this place,' said Natalie, pulling a face.

'Well, that sort of news does.' Lyn pushed back her short dark hair and, leaning back in her chair, surveyed Natalie critically.

'What are you staring at?' Natalie asked in mild alarm.

'I'm trying to see what it takes to get the great Mr Curtis to ask someone for a date.'

Natalie shrugged. 'Oh, it was just an off-the-cuff thing, that's all. Jon Bell said he had two tickets going begging. He asked Mr Curtis if he'd like them, and I just happened to be there.'

'Well, I can assure you, it's not an everyday occurrence,' said Lyn, then added, 'If you only knew how many members of staff have tried. . .'

'I suppose it's different for me,' mused Natalie.

'Why?' Lyn looked up curiously.

'Well, we're sort of related.' As Lyn put her cup down into its saucer with a noisy clatter and stared at her in amazement Natalie wished she'd kept quiet. She hadn't mentioned her connection to Adam in the time she had been at the hospital in case there were any repercussions about her having got the job in the first place, but now it seemed as if there might be speculation of another sort.

'Related? You and Mr Curtis? In what way?'

'His late wife was my first cousin. . .'

'His late wife. . .' repeated Lyn slowly, then her jaw dropped. 'You don't mean Suzanne Drummond?'

Natalie nodded. 'Yes, and you needn't bother to say it. I know we're nothing alike.'

'I wasn't going to say anything of the sort. I'm just surprised, that's all. . .and envious, and I shouldn't think for one moment that I'll be the only one around here either!' Lyn grinned. 'Oh, well, good luck to you. I had been going to ask you to come to that new Richard Gere film at the Odeon tonight, but I guess Richard Gere can't compete with Adam Curtis.'

Natalie laughed. 'Don't be silly! I'd love to see the film—I adore Richard Gere. How about tomorrow night?'

'Fine. You're on.' Lyn stood up and, draining her cup, said, 'Well, I wish I could stay and gossip, but I must fly. . .enjoy the show,' she added with a wicked grin.

Natalie watched her go, silently cursing at what had just taken place. Since starting work at the General Natalie had quickly realised what a top position Adam Curtis held, and the last thing she wanted was anyone hinting at nepotism. She had met Lyn on her first day on the theatre unit where

Lyn worked on the recovery ward, and she had immediately liked the rosy-cheeked girl with the soft Bristol accent. Now she hoped she could rely on her to be discreet.

She could, however, understand the interest Lyn had shown, for she knew only too well the sort of gossip that surrounded the private lives of the consultants in any hospital. Ruefully Natalie found herself wondering what Lyn's reaction would have been if she knew that not only was she slightly related to Adam Curtis and that he had asked her out that evening, but that she also just happened to be staying in his London home.

She finished her tea, then returned to the theatres, where she had a good two hours of preparation work for the following day's lists. There were still operations in progress as she took her seat in her office, but she knew Adam was doing a clinic in Out-patients that afternoon. She worked steadily, arranging duty rotas and planning schedules, telephoning different hospital departments to check arrangements.

The responsibility for the smooth running of three theatres rested squarely on her shoulders, and she took her work seriously, knowing full well that if anything went wrong she would be answerable. Staff shortages seemed to be the biggest problem, especially when her own staff were on leave or sick and there never seemed to be enough cover.

As she desperately tried to juggle staff rotas she made a mental note to go and see the new administrator responsible for the theatres units whom she had heard Uri Adahbi mention, and have a word with him about more staff.

Although she had worked in Theatre in her previous job, her work now at the General was on a vastly different scale, but it was a challenge, and Natalie had always been one to rise to a challenge.

When her shift was over for the day she hurried to the car park and with a sigh of relif climbed into her Mini. As she pulled out into the dense rush-hour traffic she glanced in her mirror and realised with a jolt that Adam was behind her in his dark green Daimler.

Twenty minutes later she pulled up outside Sheridan House and he drew in behind her. He followed her into the house, and as she started to climb the stairs he said, 'Can you be ready by seven?'

She stopped and, turning, looked down at him. He was standing with one hand on the newel post. 'Of course,' she replied, wondering if he was regretting his impulsive invitation.

'I thought we'd take a cab. Curtain up is at seven forty-five, then afterwards we could go somewhere for supper.'

'Oh, but. . .'

'No buts,' he smiled, that tight little smile she had come to associate with him. 'Besides, it's about time you told me what's been happening in Pitlochry.'

'What do you mean?' She stared at him.

'Well, it must have been something pretty drastic. When we spoke at the wedding you were certain you had everything you wanted right there in Scotland. I'm curious to hear what it was that made you change your mind.'

With her heart thumping painfully Natalie hurried to her room, only too conscious that he stood watching her from the foot of the stairs. She thankfully shut the door and leaned against it.

What was she going to tell him? That she had accepted his offer because it presented a professional challenge? Or because she had felt it was time to move out of the house in Pitlochry and let Kirsty run it? There were, she knew, elements of truth in both those reasons, but deep in her heart she knew the real reason was that she wanted to be near him.

But how could she admit to him that she had cherished these feelings for years, painfully burying them at the time of his marriage, only to have them resurface when she knew he had been widowed? That other relationships had paled into insigificance, and that she had always nurtured a dream that somehow she and Adam would meet again?

She was under no illusions that if she was to make such a confession Adam would think she was mad. After all, these wild longings didn't quite fit the image of a mature theatre sister at the top of her profession.

Slowly she walked across the room and, opening her wardrobe, stared at the rail of clothes, wondering what she should wear.

There had, of course, been misgivings in the time

between her applying for the job and taking up the position. She knew only too well the danger of reading too much into Adam's actions. He could quite simply have really needed a new theatre sister, spotted the potential in her, offered her the job, then extended the hospitality of his home purely through their family connections.

Carefully she lifted out a dress of emerald-green jersey silk and held it against her, studying the effect in the full-length oval mirror in the corner of the room. The colour was perfect against her hair and creamy complexion, and instinctively she knew it was right for the evening ahead.

There was, of course, on the other hand, the possibility, however remote, that Adam was interested in her, that when he had seen her at James and Kirsty's wedding he had, for the first time, seen her as a woman.

There had, however, been little evidence to substantiate that theory in the past two weeks, she thought as she pulled a rueful face at herself in the mirror, for, although they had been living in the same house, apart from at work they had seen very little of each other. Until today, that was, and, when she had least been expecting it, Adam had at last asked her out.

Maybe this too was merely a polite gesture on his part, but as Natalie peeled off her clothes and stepped under the shower she made up her mind that she would grasp the opportunity and enjoy the evening ahead.

She dressed with great care, first drawing on matching pearl-grey lingerie, then the sheerest of stockings, before stepping into the emerald-green dress. She applied a little more make-up than usual, highlighting her grey eyes and delicate cheekbones, then turned her attention to her hair.

Once the bane of her life, the shining Titian-coloured locks, she now recognised, were her crowning glory. Usually she wore it in a smooth shoulder-length bob or, when she was working, tucked inside her theatre cap, but tonight she was feeling adventurous. Carefully she plaited it into an intricate style, fastening it with a bow set with sparkling stones.

When she was finally satisfied she applied a light spray of her favourite perfume, then picked up her cape and an evening bag.

Adam was waiting for her in the hall, and as her footsteps made no sound on the thick pile carpet she had the advantage of seeing him before he saw her. Tonight, instead of the customary dark lounge suit that he wore for work, he was wearing a jacket of deep burgundy velvet, a bow-tie and a pleated white shirt with immaculately fitted black trousers.

With his thick dark hair just touched with grey, he looked achingly handsome, and in the instant that he looked up and saw her Natalie's breath caught in her throat.

For a moment he remained perfectly still, staring at her almost as if he didn't recognise her, as if he wondered who she was and what she was doing in his house.

Then the moment passed; she saw a brief flare of admiration in his dark eyes, then he moved forward and taking her cape, he moved behind her, draping it carefully round her shoulders.

'You look beautiful, Natalie,' he murmured, and as she felt his warm breath on the nape of her neck she smiled at the tone of his voice.

CHAPTER THREE

THEIR seats were in the centre of the dress circle, the best in the house, and as the orchestra played the opening chords Natalie stole a glance at Adam's profile. Even now, after working with him and staying in his house, she could hardly believe that he had actually asked her out and she was sitting beside him in a London theatre. Almost as if he sensed she was watching him he turned his head, and he gave her a brief smile before their attention was claimed by the opening number.

The show was all she had anticipated, and as they left the theatre to the reality of a wet, blustery February night Natalie felt as if her emotions had been torn apart. She wondered if it had affected Adam in the same way, and as they sat in the cab while it threaded its way through the narrow streets of London's theatre-land she again stole a glance at him.

This time, however, in contrast to before the show, when he had appeared relaxed, he seemed tense, keyed up in some way as he stared from the cab window. With a pang she wondered if he had been thinking of Suzanne, reliving some precious memory, some other theatre trip in the past, and her brother's words echoed in her brain. He had said that Adam had worshipped Suzanne, that he didn't think he had ever got over her death.

Uncomfortably Natalie shifted in her seat and tried to push James's words to the back of her mind. While she accepted that Adam had indeed adored his wife and had been devastated at her death, she also believed that time was a healer and that life had to go on. Suzanne had been dead for over three years; it was a long time, and Adam should have started to live again. Taking a deep breath, she said, 'Did you enjoy the show?'

'Yes, I did enjoy it.' He turned to look at her. 'It's an incredible experience, especially the first time.' As she raised her head questioningly he added, 'Yes, I must confess, I've seen it before.' She knew then her assumptions had been correct.

As the cab stopped before a small restaurant and he opened the door Adam smiled briefly. 'I hope you approve.' He gestured towards the restaurant. 'It could only be French, after what we've just seen.'

Natalie had been expecting something elegant and very chic, but to her pleasant surprise the bistro was friendly and cheerful, with bright red gingham cloths on the tables and a man in the corner playing an accordion, but she was still slightly on edge, knowing Adam meant to ask her about what had prompted her move to London.

It wasn't, however, until they had finished their supper and were lingering over a coffee that the inevitable question came, and when it did it was to the point.

'So, what happened to make you change your mind?' The question sounded quite casual as Adam appeared to be studying the pattern on the coffee-pot.

'To make me change my mind?' she mused, playing for time, but aware by then that he had looked up and was staring keenly at her across the table.

'Yes, Natalie, something must have happened. You were so sure that you had all you wanted in Scotland.'

'Was I?' She gave a tight little smile.

He nodded. 'You were.' He paused, but continued to stare at her, narrowing his eyes.

'I simply did as you asked and thought it over.'

'And how did you reach your decision?'

She hesitated, wondering fleetingly what he would say if she told him the truth, that she had seen his offer as the last opportunity she would ever be likely to have to be near him and discover once and for all if her feelings for him were real or the remnants of a teenage crush. Instead she said, 'I felt it was a good time to make a change. When you asked me it took me by surprise, and my first reaction was to say that I was perfectly happy with my life, but then, when I had the time to examine my feelings, I realised that for several reasons it could be a good opportunity to make some changes in my life.'

'And am I to be allowed to know those reasons?'

Suddenly, to her horror, she became aware that her hands were trembling, and in desperation she hid them beneath the table. She couldn't be certain, however, that he hadn't noticed. 'Of course,' she replied, hoping her voice sounded casual but horribly afraid that it had come out sounding strained and full of the emotion she was so trying to hide. She swallowed. 'Well, for a start, I believe I had reached the furthest I could possibly go in my career in that particular hospital. What you offered presented a challenge, and I've always been one to rise to a challenge.' She attempted a smile, but when she looked up she found his expression was serious.

'I felt there was more to your decision than that,' he said quietly. 'I felt there were personal issues involved.'

Natalie looked up wildly. Surely he didn't know? Surely he couldn't have guessed? His expression, however hadn't changed. She took another deep breath. 'Well, yes, I suppose to a certain extent that's true.' She paused, then in a rush she said, 'Now that James and Kirsty are married I feel they should have some privacy. As it is, they have my father to keep an eye on, and his health hasn't been at all good lately.'

'I didn't know that.' Adam threw her a sharp glance. 'In fact, I thought how well he looked at the wedding.'

'He put on a brave face that day, but his angina has got much worse; hence his decision to retire. Things have changed drastically in Pitlochry,' she added as if that summed up her reasons for coming to London.

Adam, however, seemed far from convinced, and as he poured more coffee he said, 'So were those your only reasons?'

'Of course. Why do you ask?' Her heart was thudding painfully. There was something about his apparent air of perceptiveness that was making her decidedly uneasy, as if he could see through to her soul.

'I got the impression that your reasons may have been even more personal than that,' he said softly. 'That there may have been a man involved. Am I wrong?'

'Quite wrong,' she answered lightly.

He smiled. 'I find it hard to believe that someone as lovely as you has no romantic attachment.'

To her horror she found herself blushing furiously at his words.

'Are you trying to tell me there isn't anyone in your life at present?' he went on relentlessly.

Desperately Natalie tried to pull herself together. Didn't she want him to know she was unattached, for heaven's sake?

She shook her head, and in what she hoped was a flippant tone she said, 'That's exactly what I'm trying to say—there's no one in my life at the moment.'

'Do I take it from that that there has been?' There was a quizzical expression in his eyes now, mingling with amusement, as if he found her embarrassment endearing.

'Of course there has. . .' she answered sharply, then trailed off, shrugging helplessly.

'But nothing serious,' he finished for her.

She shook her head. 'No, nothing serious,' she echoed.

He didn't comment further, but as he called for the bill he seemed pleased, and for one wild moment Natalie wondered if it was because he had discovered that she was unattached. He had, after all, asked her out, and Lyn Irving had implied that he never dated members of staff.

'When do you go to Brussels?' she asked suddenly.

'The day after tomorrow.' He grimaced, and she got the impression he didn't want to go.

'And how long will you be away?'

'About a week.'

They were mostly silent on the return journey to Sheridan House, but after the tension of earlier it was a comfortable silence, and Natalie found she was content just being close to him; that conversation was unnecessary.

Jane Markham had left a lamp burning in the hall for them, and as Adam helped Natalie with her cape she said, 'It's been a lovely evening, Adam; thank you.'

'It's been my pleasure,' he murmured as momentarily his fingers brushed her neck. She stiffened, holding her breath, turning her head slightly, anticipating his next move, then the magic evaporated as he said, 'It's very late, and we have another full list tomorrow. I must let you get to bed.'

She tried to answer lightly, but her pulses were still racing. 'Quite. I'm sure you wouldn't want me falling asleep on duty, or to be making mistakes,' she said.

'I wouldn't think there's any fear of that with you,' he said quietly. By this time Natalie had turned to take her cape from him, but he didn't release it immediately and there was something in his tone that made her look up. Her eyes met his, and the expression she saw there she found impossible to define.

Then he said softly, 'I'm glad you decided to come here, Natalie.'

'So am I,' she whispered. There was a long pause, and when it seemed as if he wasn't going to say more she turned away and began to climb the stairs, then as he suddenly reached out and put his hand over hers on the banister rail she stopped, her heart thudding madly.

'Natalie. . .' His voice sounded strangely husky.

'Yes. . .?'

He was silent for a long moment, then he dropped his hand. 'It's nothing. . . I'm sorry.' He turned away then, and she watched him for a moment before continuing up the stairs to her room.

Later, as she lay in bed and sleep eluded her, she went over and over in her mind the events of the evening, and her spirits soared because she knew that for the first time Adam Curtis had shown some interest in her—not just as the kid sister of his friend, the cousin of his late wife or even as his professional colleague, but as a woman. The look in his eyes had confirmed that, when for that brief moment his hand had covered hers. His touch had been almost electric and for a moment he had seemed surprised at his own reaction.

Well, maybe he was surprised, she thought as she smiled into the darkness, surprised that James's little sister had become a woman. It had seemed as if he hadn't known how to handle this unexpected development. But she could wait, she told herself, she could wait and let him get used to the situation. After all, she'd played the waiting game for so long now—waiting for Adam Curtis to recognise her existence—that a little longer wouldn't make any difference.

And now, of course, she had the distinct advantage of being near him; before, she had hardly seen him. Yes, she was more than certain she had made the right decision in coming to London.

The only person who had seemed to have doubts had been James. She had told him of her decision as they had walked the family Labradors through the hills above Loch Tummel one Sunday morning.

'Are you sure about this?' He had turned and stared at her almost in alarm, and she remembered that she had been surprised by his reaction.

'But why are you going?' He had looked worried. 'I thought you were happy here.'

'I am happy here, but I feel it's time for a change, especially career-wise.'

'Maybe. . .' He had still looked doubtful and they had walked on in silence while the dogs rooted around in the dead bracken.

Then after a while James had said, 'Natalie, I don't want you to think there isn't still a home for you here.'

'Of course I don't think that.' Her reply had been firm, but her brother had remained unconvinced, and, as they had begun their descent down the rough rocky path to the road below, the inevitable question had come.

'Does this have anything to do with Adam?' he had asked at last, and Natalie had noticed to her amusement that he looked embarrassed.

'Of course it does,' she had replied lightly. 'It has everything to do with him—after all, it was he who offered me the job.'

'I know that, but. . .'

'And he who has invited me to stay at Sheridan House as his guest until I find a place of my own.'

'He's what?' James had thrown her a sharp glance, then when she had nodded in reply he had said, 'I'm really not sure that's a good idea, Natalie.'

'Why ever not? Oh, for goodness' sake, James, I'm not a child!'

'I know, I know that,' he'd mumbled. 'But you were very keen on Adam once, you know.'

'I know.' She'd replied calmly, hoping she

sounded convincing. 'But I was little more than a child then, James. A lot has happened since then.'

'Too right it has! Including the fact that you've grown into a very beautiful young woman, and, as I said to you before, old Adam can't have failed to notice that.'

'And would that be so dreadful. . .if he had?' she had asked quietly.

At that James had looked miserable. 'He's changed, you know, Natalie; he isn't the Adam we knew in the old days.' He had hesitated. 'I would hate you to get hurt.'

She had laughed then and, patting her brother's arm, she had said, 'You really must stop worrying about me; I'm a big girl now and perfectly able to take care of myself, even in the big bad city.'

Now, as sleep still eluded her, she recalled her brother's anxieties and smilingly hugged her pillow. Adam had changed, she was the first to admit that, but a lot had happened in his life to bring about that change. She was convinced, however, that James's fears about her getting hurt were completely unfounded. Surely this evening had proved that, for wasn't she feeling happier now than she'd felt in a very long time?

The following day all thoughts of personal affairs were thrust into the background. Problems of a very different nature took precedence when Natalie found herself seriously short of staff as the theatre

teams were struck by the flu bug which had claimed
Jon Bell's wife Liz as one of its first victims.

After frantic phone calls to the nursing management Natalie finally had to accept that on top of her
own work she would have to act as Adam's scrub
nurse for that morning's list.

The first patient was a very nervous lady whom
Natalie had gone to see the previous day at the ward
sister's request to help prepare her for her
operation.

Her name was Dulcie Gale, she was forty years
old, unmarried and with a previous history of mam-
mary cysts. She had contacted her GP with what she
had thought was another cyst but which had turned
out to be a tumour. Her operation that morning was
for the removal of the tumour, which could in turn
lead to a mastectomy.

She was understandably in a highly anxious state
and had required considerable counselling. Natalie
had done her best to reassure her and to set her
mind at rest with regard to the actual operation.

'Mr Curtis is one of the finest general surgeons in
the country today,' she had explained to Dulcie as
she had sat beside her in the day-room. 'Has he
been in to see you yet?'

The woman nodded and momentarily the lines of
tension on her face eased a little. 'Yes, he came this
morning. He was very kind, and he told me he
would only take the breast away as a very last
resort.'

'That's absolutely right, and you must believe it,'

said Natalie firmly. 'Now, when you come down to Theatre in the morning I shall be there waiting for you. I've put you first on the list so you won't have too much hanging around. Have you got any questions you want to ask me?'

'Will I be sick when I come round?' Dulcie looked anxious again. 'I had my appendix out a few years ago and I was horribly sick then.'

'Modern anaesthetics have improved tremendously,' replied Natalie, 'but I'll make a note of what you've told me and I'll have a word with the anaesthetist so he is aware of your problem. He'll be in to see you anyway, and he'll probably be able to give you something to prevent nausea. Now I want you to try and get a good night's sleep.' She paused as she saw Dulcie's expression. 'Don't worry, they'll give you a sedative to help you,' she added.

After she had left the patient she had had a word with the ward sister, who had confirmed that the patient was also asthmatic and that salbutamol would be included with her premedication to obtain good lung expansion.

Now, as she prepared the theatre for the first operation of the day, Natalie's thoughts were with Dulcie Gale, and as Adam arrived to scrub up and change into his green tunic, trousers and boots she slipped into the anaesthetic-room just as the orderlies wheeled in the patient.

'Hello, Dulcie,' Natalie smiled, and was pleased

to see that Dulcie looked relaxed and stress-free after her premed.

'Hello.' Dulcie looked puzzled for a moment, then she smiled faintly. 'Oh, it's you, Sister—I didn't recognise you in green.'

'I promised I'd be here, didn't I? Now tell me, did you get a good night's sleep?'

'Yes, as a matter of fact I did.'

'Good, now you just relax and leave all the worrying to us.'

'Sister. . .?'

'Yes, Dulcie?' Natalie had turned away, but she paused.

'Will you be there while. . .you know. . .?'

'Yes, I shall be there.'

'You won't let them. . .you know, unless they really have to. . .will you?'

'No, I won't, I promise.' Natalie smiled reassuringly. 'Not unless they really have to. Here's Mr Bell to see you now—you've met him, haven't you?' Leaving Jon Bell to chat briefly to Dulcie before he administered the anaesthetic, she slipped back into Theatre.

Adam seemed surprised to find that she was acting as scrub nurse.

'There was no one else,' she said. 'Our cover during sickness and holidays is quite inadequate.'

'This chap Lomax is the one you want to tell,' said Adam.

'I fully intend to,' replied Natalie firmly, then she instructed a relief nurse to return to the scrub-room for touching her face after scrubbing up. 'I need eyes in the back of my head—it's not the way I want my theatre run.'

'Well, you should get your chance to complain at the staff meeting at lunchtime,' said Adam as he moved towards the table. 'Ah, Miss Gale, isn't it? Right, Sister, shall we get started?'

As the operation progressed Natalie felt her anger subside, and before long she was totally absorbed in what was happening on the operating table and had quite forgotten her earlier frustrations over staff.

She enjoyed watching Adam work, especially when there were students present and he explained what he was doing. His deep voice, together with the deft movements of his strong hands, had an almost mesmerising effect, and she had to force herself to concentrate on her own duties, which included passing instruments to Adam or his assistant, Dr Farmer, accounting for the number of swabs used and the administration of the diathermy machine to control the bleeding.

She watched carefully as the tumour was removed and Adam probed the surrounding tissue for any signs of malignancy, then at last he straightened up. 'I'm as sure as I can be at this stage that the breast is healthy,' he said. 'A frozen section will of course tell us more, but I'm very optimistic that this little monster is harmless'.

Dulcie Gale remained in the hands of the anaesthetist while the tumour was taken to the pathology lab for biopsy. The report was then phoned through to the theatre from the lab by a senior technician.

Natalie found herself holding her breath as she watched Adam's face while he listened to the report, then she breathed a sigh of relief for Dulcie when he said, 'All's clear, Sister. We have some suturing to do.'

While his assistant was stitching the wound and Natalie prepared the dressing pack the student nurse who had been watching the operation asked Adam what would have happened if the biopsy had proved malignant.

'Almost certainly I would have had to perform a mastectomy,' he replied. 'That would have been followed by chemotherapy to eradicate any further spread of the malignancy, then a course of tamoxifen. The patient would then, some weeks later, have been fitted with a prosthesis, an artificial breast.' He looked down at Dulcie Gale as he spoke. 'Happily in this case that won't be necessary.'

At the conclusion of the morning's list, after Natalie had changed and gone back to her office, Adam put his head round the door. 'What's the staff situation for this afternoon's list, Sister?'

She pulled a face. 'Not a lot better, I'm afraid.'

'Are you coming over to the postgraduate centre for this meeting?'

'If it means having my say about staff shortages then yes, certainly. Will you be there?' She looked up enquiringly. It was rare for consultants to attend staff meetings.

'You bet,' he replied grimly, then, catching sight of her expression, he added, 'Where the running of the theatre and my staff are concerned I make it my business to be involved. I'll walk over there with you if you're ready.'

She took her navy blue cape from a peg behind the office door and wrapped it around her. They had to cross the hospital grounds to the postgraduate centre, and as the cold February wind whipped around them she was glad of the warmth of the thick woollen cape.

The hall was very full, but they managed to find two vacant seats, although it meant Adam sitting in the row behind Natalie. She had had little opportunity to meet many of the management team since joining the staff of the General, and when she studied the personnel sitting on the platform she realised she only knew her immediate nursing manager and her deputy. The meeting proved to be rather noisy and at one point became very overheated as members of staff had their say about crucial issues such as gradings and postings.

When the subject changed to staff shortages everyone wanted to join in, and Natalie had to be patient before she was finally invited to have her say. She stood up and put her case clearly and firmly, stating that theatre staffing was running on a shoestring and she feared the consequences in terms of patient care and lengthening waiting lists.

She finished speaking amid nods and murmurs of

agreement from her colleagues, and as she sat down a man on the management team stood up to reply.

He was of medium height and slightly built, with sandy hair and a hooded but penetrating gaze. It was difficult to guess his age, but she judged him to be somewhere in his thirties. His features, although not handsome, were arresting, with a high-bridged nose and curious yellow-green eyes, and as he fixed her with his stare she shivered slightly.

'I don't believe we've met. . . Sister?' he began, and his accent was North Country.

'Fraser; Natalie Fraser,' she replied firmly. For some reason her hands had become clammy, which was of course quite ridiculous, because she certainly wasn't afraid of this man, whoever he was.

'Well, Sister Fraser, I gather you're new at the General?' He seemed to be summing her up with his gaze.

'That's quite correct,' she answered.

'And may I ask exactly how long you have been with us?'

'Just two weeks.'

'Really? To me that seems a very short time to see how things work here. Perhaps it would be better if you were to give it a bit longer before rushing in and trying to change everything.'

'I don't need any longer.' Natalie's reply was almost defiant. The colour had risen to her cheeks at the faintly sarcastic tone he had adopted. 'It doesn't take time for me to know whether or not I'm short of staff to run a theatre. We have just enough. That's .fine, until someone is sick or, as happened today, when three people are sick and there is no one to take their place—then we have problems.'

'So what are you saying, Sister?' He raised his eyebrows.

'Quite simply that we need more cover.'

'And if I tell you, quite simply, that there's no money for more staff, what is your answer to that?'

A hush had descended on the hall, but Natalie was determined not to be intimidated by this man. 'My answer would be that that is your problem, not mine.'

There was a ripple of applause and laughter in the hall, and the man's eyes narrowed slightly.

'I'm sorry,' Natalie went on, 'but you asked what I was saying, and I told you. My problem is lack of staff, just as much as yours is lack of money.'

As she sat down Adam leaned forward. 'Well done,' he murmured.

'Who is he anyway?' whispered Natalie over her shoulder.

'Roger Lomax, the new administrator.'

'Good; perhaps we'll get something done now,' she murmured back.

'I wouldn't count on it,' replied Adam cryptically.

CHAPTER FOUR

AFTER the meeting Adam disappeared with his secretary in the direction of his office, and Natalie made her way to the staff canteen for a quick sandwich.

A glance around the crowded area did not reveal any of her team, so she took her lunch to a table in the window that overlooked the hospital grounds and the busy London streets beyond. She sighed as she peeled the wrapping from her sandwiches and gazed out at the bleak February day and the endless drab buildings. She was finding it very strange adapting to city life, having lived in the country ever since she was born. She missed the open spaces, the hills and lochs and the wide endless skies, and, although she found certain aspects of life in London new and exciting, she knew it would take a long time to settle completely.

At the next table a group of noisy medical students were discussing details of their forthcoming rag week. Natalie had succeeded in shutting their chatter from her mind, but in the process she had become so lost in her own private thoughts that she started as someone suddenly balanced a tray on the corner of her table and began unloading it.

'The usual lunchtime rabble in here, I see. Not a lot of space, is there?'

With a jolt she realised it was Roger Lomax—
just about the last person in the hospital she would
have chosen to have lunch with at that particular
time. But it seemed she was to have no say in the
matter, for, without asking if she minded, he
propped his tray against the table leg, then sat down
in the chair opposite.

He proceeded to tuck into his pie and chips with
great relish, and Natalie was just wondering how
quickly she could make her escape when he said
suddenly, 'Quite a meeting, wasn't it?'

She stared at him, amazed by his offhand manner,
then she said tartly, 'Well, it will have been if it
achieves anything. If it doesn't it will have been a
complete and utter waste of time—as, in my experience, many staff meetings are.'

He set his fork down and with his head tilted
slightly to one side he studied her. 'And where does
that experience come from? Would I be right in
assuming north of the Border?'

She nodded. 'You would.'

'I recognised the accent the moment you started
attacking me in there. No, don't apologise. . . I
appreciate a woman who can sustain a good
argument.'

'I wasn't going to apologise,' replied Natalie
quickly, aware, however, that colour had suffused
her cheeks and hating herself for it.

'So what part of Scotland are you from?' he
carried on, nonplussed by her remark.

'Pitlochry.'

This time he set both his knife and fork down and stared at her in apparent amazement. 'You don't say!'

'You know Pitlochry?' She was curious now, hungry for any link with home.

'Do I know Pitlochry. . .?' He repeated her question wonderingly. 'I should say I do. I spent every holiday there when I was a boy, and a good few since. . .' a faraway look had come into his heavy-lidded eyes '. . . the old salmon leap. . .fishing in Loch Rannoch. . .trips to Aviemore.'

She leaned forward with interest as she realised he had been telling the truth, and, probably because her thoughts had been on her home only moments before, her attitude towards this previously abrasive man softened slightly.

'My father was a GP in Pitlochry,' she said, then added, 'My brother has taken over the practice now.'

'Is that a fact? I probably met your father. I had to have treatment once after a fall when I was rock-climbing in the area and busted my ankle.' He shook his head. 'This really is a coincidence. We must get together some time, Sister Fraser—or may I call you Natalie?'

She glanced up sharply, surprised that he had remembered her name, but before she had the chance to either agree or refuse he carried on talking.

'Yes, we really must get together and swap stories of the Highlands.'

She smiled, thinking there wasn't anything she'd rather do at that moment than talk about her home. They were silent for a while as he ate his meal, then Natalie asked a question that had niggled at the back of her mind ever since she had heard him speak at the meeting. 'Talking of accents,' she said, and he looked up enquiringly, 'I can't quite identify yours.'

He began stirring his tea and didn't immediately reply, then he said, 'Oh, I'm a bit of a hybrid. My father was Irish, my mother came from the Midlands and I've spent most of my life in the Liverpool area.'

'And now you've moved down here to London. Have you found it difficult to settle?'

He shrugged. 'Not really.'

'Did you have problems with accommodation?'

'No, I'm living in a flat here at the hospital at the moment, but I hope to be moving into my own place soon—how about you?'

'Oh, I've been looking for a flat, but everything is so expensive.'

'So are you living in as well?' He glanced at her curiously. 'I haven't seen you around the quarters.'

Natalie shook her head. 'No. . . I'm staying with a. . .a friend.'

'Another member of staff?'

'Yes, yes, that's right.' There was no way she wanted to tell him she was staying with Adam Curtis. Apart from the fact that she wanted as few people as possible to know of the family connection, she had the feeling that Roger Lomax would certainly put the wrong interpretation on the situation.

'So do you think you're going to be happy here at the General?'

'I should think so—if I get the staff I want to run the theatre as I think it should be run.' She allowed a cryptic note of amusement into her tone.

He raised his eyebrows, a wry expression on his rather pale features. 'There's not a lot I can do about that. Oh, I know everyone blames me,' he said as he saw her expression, 'but I'm only doing my job, the same as you, or Adam Curtis, for that matter. I get a set amount of money in my budget and I have to allocate it. When it's gone, it's gone.' He shrugged again, and in spite of her earlier anger Natalie found herself nodding in agreement. Then, glancing at her watch, she sighed and stood up. 'I'll have to go—we've another list starting shortly.'

For a moment she thought he was going to say more, to detain her in some way as he held her gaze with his penetrating eyes, but he merely nodded. 'See you around, Natalie.'

The afternoon proved to be every bit as frantic as the morning had been, but this time at least Natalie had a scrub nurse for Adam, so she was able to concentrate on her own duties.

It was while they were clearing up at the end of the day that Adam casually asked if she would be at home for dinner that night.

She turned from the steriliser in surprise. It was the first time at the hospital that he had made any reference to the fact that she was staying at Sheridan House. She glanced round, but there didn't seem to be anyone else in earshot. 'I should think so, yes,' she replied.

Then, remembering her cinema trip with Lyn, she was about to add that she would be going out afterwards when Adam said, 'I have to go out later in the evening, so we shall be dining early, but I thought it might be nice to have dinner together as it's my last night at home for a while.'

'Of course.' She stared at him. 'You're off to Brussels in the morning. In that case, yes, I'll definitely be there for dinner.' She suddenly felt pleased that he had asked her, that he wanted her company, and she wondered if the time they had shared the previous evening had anything to do with it.

She arrived home before Adam and was greeted in the hall by Jane Markham's son, Timothy. He was a quiet, well-behaved little boy who looked incredibly like his mother and even seemed to have inherited her short-sightedness. On the occasions Natalie had seen him about the house he had always seemed to have his nose in a book. Now he appeared to have been waiting for her to arrive home.

'Hello, Timothy.' Natalie closed the front door behind her and smiled as he scrambled up from the stairs where he had been sitting. 'What have you got there?' she asked as she spied the inevitable book under his arm.

'I got it from school—it's a prize,' he replied earnestly, his eyes shining behind his glasses. 'Look, it's all about making models from wax.'

Natalie set her bag down and took the book. 'I say, well done—what a super book,' she said as she turned the glossy pages. 'What did you get it for?'

'Technology design,' he replied solemnly.

'Whatever's that?' gasped Natalie with a laugh.

'I think it was called handicrafts when I was at school.' Jane Markham suddenly appeared from the kitchen, wiping her hands on a navy and white striped apron.

Natalie laughed and handed the book back to Timothy.

'Good evening, Miss Fraser,' said Jane, then, looking at her son, she added, 'I hope you're not making a nuisance of yourself, Timothy.'

'Of course he isn't,' said Natalie swiftly. 'He was just showing me his prize.'

'He's very proud of that,' admitted his mother.

'I should think so too; he has every right to be.'

'Is Mr Curtis with you?' asked Jane suddenly.

Natalie shook her head. 'No, but he shouldn't be long. He said he'll be going out later but that he'd be home for dinner tonight. And of course he's off to Brussels in the morning.'

'You'll be dining with him, Miss Fraser?'

'I will.' Natalie had begun to climb the stairs, but she paused. 'Oh, and Jane, please call me Natalie.

Every time you call me Miss Fraser I expect my maiden aunt to appear!'

Jane smiled. 'Very well.'

Timothy looked up suddenly. 'Are you going to Brussels as well?' he asked Natalie.

She laughed and shook her head. 'I should be so lucky!'

'Mr Curtis doesn't want to go,' said Timothy solemnly.

'Timothy. . .' began his mother, a warning note in her voice.

'He doesn't,' her son carried on emphatically. 'He told me so this morning. . .he said he'd much rather stay here. I 'spect he meant because of Miss Fraser being here.'

Natalie turned and stared at him. 'Whatever do you mean?'

He shrugged and began turning the pages of his book again. 'Well, if I had a friend to stay I'd want to be with them. . . I wouldn't want to go off somewhere.'

Natalie smiled then and Jane shrugged helplessly. 'I'm sorry,' she said. 'You must forgive Timothy. It's so rare for Mr Curtis to have anyone to stay that when he does it's a bit of a novelty.' She watched as her son crossed the hall to the passage that led to their own quarters. 'And I must admit he does seem to have taken a shine to you.' She looked round again and saw that Natalie was staring at her, and she must have realised what she had said. 'Oh, I'm sorry—I meant Timothy, not Mr Curtis!' She put her hand to her mouth, then smiled again. 'On the other hand, I'm sure Mr Curtis has enjoyed your company. I sometimes think he's such a lonely man, in spite of. . .' She trailed off as if she was embarrassed by what she had been going to say, then to cover her confusion she asked, 'Did you say you were related in some way?'

'Only by marriage. His wife and I were cousins,' explained Natalie, then asked, 'Were you here when Mrs Curtis was alive?'

'No, we came a few months after her death.' Jane hesitated for a moment. 'Mr Curtis was very strange then; he used to shut himself in his study for hours on end. . .' She fell silent as if reflecting on the past, then, suddenly straightening her shoulders as if she realised she shouldn't be gossiping about her employer, she said, 'Well, this won't do. At this rate Mr Curtis will be home and there'll be no dinner.'

As Jane hurried back to the kitchen Natalie carried on thoughtfully up the stairs.

Her bedroom, which had its own private bathroom, was as quietly elegant as the rest of Sheridan House. The soft, thick carpets were pale blue, while the large double bed was covered in a rich spread of royal-blue satin with an over-cover of cream Nottingham lace. The décor and curtains were also cream, with a thin stripe of royal blue, and the furnishings were in dark oak. Ever since her arrival Natalie had wondered if the choices had been

Adam's, Suzanne's or even a firm of interior designers'.

She ran herself a bath, adding a liberal quantity of foaming bath cream, then, peeling off her clothes, she stepped into the scented water and with a sigh lay back in the soft foam and felt the tensions of the day drift away. She knew if she wasn't very careful she could find herself becoming too accustomed to the high degree of luxury at Sheridan House.

She was also under no illusions that probably the only reason she was there was her relationship to Suzanne. Without that she would have been slumming it at the nurses' home.

She smiled to herself as she sponged her legs with the velvety foam and recalled how Timothy had thought Adam didn't want to go to Brussels because he wanted to stay with her. But a little later, as she critically surveyed her clothes in the wardrobe, she once again found herself taking pains over her appearance.

Finally she selected a pair of culottes in a soft silky material with a matching top in grey and black print, which did wonders for her hair and creamy complexion. As she brushed her hair into its usual shiny bob she suddenly recalled Adam's expression the previous evening when he had watched her walk down the stairs, and on a sudden impulse she swept her hair back from her face, securing it behind her ears with two marcasite combs. The result was quite dramatic, enough to evoke the desired reaction from Adam when she joined him for a pre-dinner drink.

She found him standing in front of the fire, his drink in one hand, and he appeared to be studying the painting above the mantelpiece. She must have made a small sound as she entered the room, for he spoke, but without turning. 'I never tire of this painting,' he said. 'Whenever I think I know all there is to know, I find some new aspect that I'd previously overlooked.

'It's one of my favourites as well,' replied Natalie.

'Really?' He turned as if in sudden pleasure that their tastes should coincide, and it was then, when he first caught sight of her, that that unmistakable look of admiration entered his eyes, and Natalie felt the warm colour touch her cheeks.

'You should wear your hair that way more often,' he said softly. 'It shows off your bone-structure.'

'Trust a surgeon to say that!' She laughed, but nervously, for there had been something about his comment, or the way that he'd said it, that had unnerved her slightly, set her pulses racing. Then the moment was lost and he was asking her what she would like to drink.

While he was pouring her a Martini she took the opportunity to study him. He was casually dressed in a silk shirt of deep turquoise and charcoal-grey close-fitting trousers. It was unusual to see him dressed like this, for while he was working he either wore his green theatre uniform or an immaculate dark suit, and on the occasions she had seen him dressed ready to attend some function he had, of course, been in evening dress.

She decided she liked the new image; it made him look more modern and somehow younger. For a moment she cast her mind back to the time when she had been a lovelorn teenager and had so worshipped him. Whatever would he think if he knew that now? So much had happened in the years since then that it was hard to believe they were the same people.

He turned from the sideboard and crossed the room, then as he handed her the glass for a brief moment his fingers touched hers.

Natalie was so intent on not spilling her drink that she didn't look up immediately, but when he didn't withdraw his hand she raised her eyes to his.

He was frowning slightly, but there was an expression on his face that she found vaguely familiar. It was the same expression she had seen the previous evening when he had helped her with her cape, an expression she had found impossible to define. Then it was gone, in the same instant that he withdrew his hand, and he was raising his own glass in a toast.

'I think we should drink to good health, the end of the flu epidemic and the return of our staff,' he said.

'I'll certainly drink to that,' she replied.

'I was impressed with the way you spoke up at the staff meeting.'

'Oh, I can speak up when I want to,' she said, tilting her chin defiantly, 'especially when it's something I feel strongly about. And, believe me, I feel strongly about being under-staffed.'

Adam nodded. 'I agree, staff shortages could generate mistakes, and when that happens we are to blame.'

'Exactly,' Natalie warmed to the theme, 'but if we have unsympathetic people in charge of the purse-strings I don't see what we can do.'

'You mean people like Roger Lomax?' Adam grimaced, his expression giving away precisely what he thought of the new administrator.

'Actually, he wasn't so bad as I had at first thought,' replied Natalie.

'I thought he was rude and arrogant,' said Adam

'So did I in the meeting, but later, when I spoke to him, he seemed a little more friendly.'

'Where did you see him later?'

'He joined me for lunch in the canteen. We talked about Scotland—apparently he knows Pitlochry very well, spends his holidays there and, well,' she raised her eyebrows expressively, 'anyone with such good taste as that can't be all bad. . .' She laughed, and glanced up as Jane suddenly appeared in the doorway to tell them that dinner was served.

They took their places at the oval Regency table in the dining-room, and Jane brought their first course, which turned out to be some of her excellent fish soup.

'This is quite delicious,' said Natalie after Jane had left the room.

'I know; Jane's an absolute treasure,' replied

Adam as he broke a bread roll. 'I hope she never wants to leave—I don't know what I'd do without her. The thought of finding a replacement is a nightmare.'

'Is it likely that she may want to leave?' asked Natalie, then added, 'She seems happy here.'

'Yes, I think she is.' He paused reflectively. 'A little while ago there was a man in her life and I did wonder then, but I rather gathered that he didn't get along with Timothy, and, as Timothy is the most important thing in Jane's life. . .' He shrugged, leaving the sentence unfinished.

'What happened to Timothy's father?' Natalie looked up, suddenly curious about Adam's housekeeper and her child. 'Are he and Jane divorced?'

Adam shook his head. 'No, Jane was never married. I believe she's had a struggle to bring the boy up single-handedly.'

'She tells me she's been with you for quite a while,' said Natalie thoughtfully.

'That's correct. She came here soon after Suzanne's death. I'd paid off the other staff by then and was on my own apart from a daily cleaning woman.'

'Did you have many staff?' She glanced at him curiously as she spoke. It was the first time he had voluntarily mentioned Suzanne.

'More than we needed.' He answered abruptly and his features tightened, leaving Natalie once again convinced that the subject of his late wife was still too painful for him to discuss.

Towards the end of their meal, while they were talking about James and Kirsty, Adam suddenly brought the conversation round to his trip to Brussels the following day.

'It's a bit of a nuisance, coming at this particular time,' he said as he helped himself to a piece of Brie and a handful of white grapes.

Natalie found herself wanting to ask him what he meant and why this particular time should have any significance, but before she could put the question into words he explained, 'I feel that, as you're a guest in my house, I should be here——'

'Oh, please don't worry about me,' she broke in quickly. 'Honestly, Adam, I shall be perfectly all right. Jane and Timothy are here. . .'

'But you're new to London. . .'

She laughed, silencing him with a raised hand. 'I'm fine, really I am—why, already I'm beginning to make friends. There's Lyn Irving; she's been very kind—oh, and I've joined the hospital social club.'

'Even so, I promised James I'd keep an eye on you, but then I didn't know about Brussels.'

'I don't know!' she sighed. 'I sometimes think that brother of mine imagines I'm still a child.'

'It's only natural that he should be concerned; he's probably afraid you'll get into undesirable company.' Adam laughed then and it gave him an almost boyish look.

'I should be so lucky,' said Natalie, pulling a face and silently wondering what Adam would say if he knew of the conversation she had had with her brother before leaving Pitlochry when he had implied that he was worried about her staying with Adam. They had almost finished dinner when Adam glanced at his watch and Natalie remembered he'd said he had to go out; then at that moment there came a light tap on the door and Jane appeared.

'I'm sorry to bother you, Mr Curtis,' she said, 'but there's a phone call.'

He stood up with a sigh, throwing down his napkin. 'Very well, Jane. Who is it?'

'Oh, it isn't for you, it's for Miss Fraser.'

Natalie looked up in surprise, and Adam, who had started to leave the table, stopped abruptly.

'It's a Mr Roger Lomax,' explained Jane.

CHAPTER FIVE

ADAM stared at Natalie while she got slowly to her feet, wiping her mouth with her napkin.

'I can't imagine how he knew where I was,' she said as she felt the tell-tale colour tinge her cheeks, then as she left the room she added almost defensively, 'I haven't told anyone where I'm staying.'

She took the call in Adam's study, using the phone on his desk. Lifting the receiver almost gingerly, she said, 'Hello?'

'Hello, Natalie.'

'Is there anything wrong?' she asked, thinking that Roger must be ringing on a hospital matter.

'No,' he replied shortly. 'Why should there be?'

'I was wondering why you were phoning me here and how you knew where I was.'

'Oh, I make it my business to know these things,' he said smoothly, then before she had time to say anything else he launched straight in. 'I was ringing to see if you'd come out with me tomorrow night. We could try a new pub I've discovered in Chiswick. I was going to ask you in the morning, but I've checked the rotas and I see you're off duty.'

He'd caught her completely unawares, and for a moment she was lost for words.

'Natalie? Are you still there?' There was a trace of impatience in his tone now.

'Yes.'

'Well, will you come?'

'Well, I. . .'

'Oh, come on now! I feel we got off to a bad start—at least let me put that right. Besides, I want to talk about Pitlochry.'

She took a deep breath. 'I'm sorry, Roger, I don't think so,' she heard herself reply.

There was a silence on the other end, then he said, 'Is there any particular reason?'

'What do you mean?'

'Well, are you attached? Is there someone else?'

She gripped the receiver more tightly. He was nothing if not blunt. 'Well, not exactly. . .'

'Then why not?'

'I'm sorry, but I really don't want to get involved.'

'I'm not asking you to get involved, simply to have a drink.' He sighed, and she wished she could hang up or just tell him to go away. There really wasn't any way she wanted to start any sort of relationship with Roger Lomax.

When she remained silent he said, 'Listen, have you joined the hospital social club?'

'Yes, I have,' she admitted, then immediately wondered if she'd said the right thing.

'In that case, maybe I'll see you in there some time for a drink.'

'Yes, maybe you will,' she said, relieved that the conversation seemed to be at an end.

She hung up thankfully, stared at the receiver before replacing it, then slowly returned to where Adam was waiting for her in the dining-room.

He raised his eyebrows as she sat down again. 'Whatever did he want?' he asked. 'Is there anything wrong in Theatre?'

She shook her head and gave a nervous laugh. 'No, nothing like that. He rang to ask me out,' she said with a shrug.

There was silence for a long moment, the only sound in the room the crackling of a log in the hearth before it split and fell apart, sending sparks shooting up the chimney.

Then Adam said, 'Did he, indeed?' He spoke softly, and there was an edge to his voice that Natalie hadn't heard before.

She threw him an apprehensive glance and saw that the dark brows were drawn together in an uncompromising frown.

'How did he know you were here?' he said at last.

'I asked him that, and he said he made it his business to find out.'

'Huh! I bet he did.' He stood up and walked to the mantelpiece, then turned to face her again. 'I'm sorry, Natalie but I think you should be very careful. There's something about that man I just don't like.'

She smiled then. 'You sound just like big brother James. But I shouldn't think Roger Lomax is as bad as all that.'

For a moment they faced each other across the table, and Natalie found herself wishing that

Adam's sudden concern had arisen through jealousy, but she very much doubted that that was the
case. It was more likely that he really had promised
James to keep an eye on her and not let her fall into
undesirable company.

It seemed, however, that she wasn't to find out,
for at that moment Jane appeared again, this time
to inform Adam that the cab he had ordered had
arrived.

With a smothered exclamation he glanced at his
watch, and with a muttered apology to Natalie he
disappeared upstairs.

She sat on at the table, wondering where he was
going that evening, then when she heard him come
back downstairs and the front door shut behind him
she stood up and with a sigh went to get ready for
her trip to the cinema with Lyn.

Natalie enjoyed her evening; the film was excellent and Lyn Irving was very good company. After
the performance they went to a wine bar for a drink,
then both went to the tube station, but caught trains
going in opposite directions.

By the time Natalie reached her stop it was really
quite late and she was glad she only had a couple of
hundred yards to walk to Sheridan House.

She was only a short distance from the house
when a cab drew up at the front entrance. She
guessed it was Adam also arriving home. Her heart
leapt and she quickened her pace so that they would
arrive together, but as he stepped out of the cab he
turned and helped someone else to alight.

Natalie, who was on the opposite side of the road, stopped and watched, then when she saw that the other person was a woman she instinctively stepped back into the shadows so that Adam wouldn't see her if he happened to look up.

For a moment the couple were illuminated in a circle of light from the overhead street-lamp, and Natalie, pressed against the cold railings of the house opposite, had a clear view of the woman. She was tall, almost as tall as Adam, with a mass of blonde hair that cascaded down her back. Her slim figure was accentuated by her tight black velvet trousers, white frilled blouse and her fitted black jacket threaded with silver that sparkled in the light as she moved.

As Natalie watched Adam paid the cab driver, then casually put his hand beneath the woman's elbow and guided her up the steps of Sheridan House. He unlocked the door and stepped aside to allow the woman to enter, and as she passed him she lifted her head and kissed him lightly on the lips. Before he closed the door Adam glanced up and down the road, then seemed to look directly at Natalie.

She shrank further back into the shadows, remaining there for a good ten minutes after Adam had closed the door. Suddenly she felt cold and miserable. Who was the woman? She looked as if she knew Adam very well. Slowly it began to dawn on Natalie that she had probably been very naïve where Adam was concerned. Because of the

remarks James had made about his having worshipped Suzanne and never having got over her
death she had innocently assumed there was no
other woman in his life. Well, it looked as if she'd
been wrong. It looked as if Adam could be very
much involved.

Only when she considered it safe to do so did she
venture across the road, quietly mounting the steps
and opening the front door with as little sound as
possible. The last thing she wanted was to encounter
either Adam or his glamorous companion.

Soundlessly she closed the front door, then
realised that the drawing-room door was slightly
open. Music was softly playing and as she tiptoed
across the hall she heard a woman's light laugh.

She was halfway up the stairs when Adam's voice
suddenly halted her.

'So it's you, Natalie,' he said. 'I wondered who it
was trying to creep in.'

Guiltily she turned and looked down at him. She
hadn't switched on the landing light and there was
only the table lamp that Jane always left burning in
the hall. Adam had his back to the light, so she was
unable to see his expression.

'I didn't want to disturb you,' she mumbled,
glancing at the drawing-room door, which was wide
open now.

'I hadn't realised you were out,' he said quietly.
'You didn't say you were going.'

She shrugged, wondering why it should matter to
him, then very quietly, so that there was no chance

of the woman in the drawing-room overhearing, he said, 'Have you been with Lomax?'

For a moment she didn't think she'd heard him correctly, then when she realised what he had said she opened her mouth to hotly deny it. At that moment, however, the woman in the drawing-room called out.

'Adam, darling, where are you?' Her voice was husky, and from its tone it was perfectly obvious that she didn't know he was talking to anyone.

Natalie stared at him, then when she realised he was still waiting for her reply she swallowed. Then something seemed to snap inside her. 'What if I have?' she said through gritted teeth. 'Honestly, Adam, I really can't see that it's any business of yours.' With that she turned and ran up the remaining stairs, leaving him standing in the hall, watching her.

She spent a troubled night, miserably wondering about the blonde woman and just how much she might mean to Adam. She felt hurt that he had said he'd wanted to have dinner with her when all the while he had been planning to meet this other woman later that same evening.

By the morning, however, she had calmed down, and as she showered and dressed she regretted what she had said to Adam. Really she was grateful to him for his influence in helping her to get the job and for his kindness in allowing her to stay in his home. And in all fairness he didn't know how she felt about him. What he did at Sheridan House and who he chose to bring there weren't anything to do with her.

She decided she would go down and see him before he left for the airport, as she would hate for him to leave with any misunderstanding between them

The house seemed very quiet, and when she investigated she found that the ground-floor rooms were all empty. She frowned and wandered back into the dining-room, and was just about to help herself to toast and coffee when Jane came into the room.

'Oh, Jane, there you are.' Natalie looked up from the sideboard and paused with the coffee-pot in her hand. 'Do you know where Mr Curtis is?'

'Mr Curtis? Oh, he's gone. He left about half an hour ago.'

Natalie felt a sharp stab of disappointment. 'But I thought he wasn't leaving until eight-thirty.'

'He wasn't, but because of the weather he decided to give himself more time to get through the traffic.'

'The weather?' Natalie turned towards the window, and for the first time realised that it was quite foggy outside.

'Was there something important?' asked Jane.

'Something important?' repeated Natalie vaguely, still trying to overcome her unexpected feeling of frustration at not being able to speak to Adam.

'Yes,' replied Jane patiently. 'You sounded as if you particularly wanted to see Mr Curtis before he went.'

'Oh, I'm sorry, Jane. It was nothing really. Just a slight misunderstanding that I wanted to put right, that's all.'

Jane nodded as if she knew exactly what Natalie meant, then after she'd established the fact that Natalie didn't want any breakfast she began clearing the dishes from the sideboard. She was about to leave the room when she suddenly stopped in the doorway, hesitated, then said, 'I'm really lucky to have Mr Curtis as an employer.' And when Natalie looked up from the table in surprise she continued, 'He's been so kind. . .there can't be many men in his position who would have taken on me and a young child the way he did.'

'I'm sure you've more than made up for it,' said Natalie kindly. 'He was only saying last night that he didn't know what he'd do without you.'

'Did he really?' Jane's face, already shiny from the heat in the kitchen, flushed with pleasure, then she said, 'I have to go into hospital in a week's time and he knows I've been worrying about Timothy. Just before he left this morning he came into the kitchen and told me I wasn't to worry. He said he'd be back from Brussels by then and that he'd make sure he'd be in the house that night with Timothy.'

Natalie looked up with concern. 'I hope it's nothing serious, Jane.'

'No, only a D and C, but I've been told I'll have to stay in overnight.'

Natalie nodded understandingly, and Jane hesitated before coninuing. 'I've been having lots of problems recently, and my doctor sent me to see someone at the hospital, who said I should have a D and C. I've been a bit worried that it will be Mr Curtis who does the op,' she said, then when she saw Natalie's expression she went on hastily, 'Oh, don't get me wrong; I've heard he's a brilliant surgeon, but I'd be embarrassed, with him being my employer. Do you know what I mean?' she asked anxiously.

'There would be no need for you to feel embarrassed in any way,' replied Natalie firmly, but then she added kindly, 'but yes, I do understand what you mean. However, you needn't have any fears on that score, Jane.'

'Why, what do you mean?' Jane still looked dubious.

'Well, Mr Curtis is a general surgeon. A gynaecologist will do your D and C.'

'Oh, I see.' Jane looked relieved. 'Well, I'm glad about that, but I'm very grateful for Mr Curtis offering to be here with Timothy that night.'

'Well, I'll do anything I can to help as well,' said Natalie. 'I should think I'll still be here then, unless I miraculously find the flat I want in the meantime.'

'Oh, I hope you won't be leaving us too soon,' said Jane. 'Timothy and I have got so used to you being here now, and I'm sure Mr Curtis enjoys your company.'

Natalie laughed. 'Oh, I don't know about that.'

'Well, all I can say is he's been happier lately than I've ever known him.'

'I would think that's just coincidence, and certainly nothing to do with me,' replied Natalie briskly as she stood up.

At that moment the telephone rang in the hall and Jane put the dishes down again and hurried to answer it. Natalie followed her, as she intended going up to her room to get ready to do some shopping.

'It's for you,' said Jane, turning from the hall table and handing her the receiver. Because she had been thinking about him, for one moment Natalie wondered if it could be Adam ringing from the airport, and almost eagerly she spoke into the mouthpiece.

To her disappointment it was her nursing manager, the only person at the hospital who officially had her telephone number.

'Natalie, I'm sorry, but do you think you could come in? Three more have gone down with flu and already Casualty are sending up emergencies because of this wretched fog.'

Natalie sighed, abandoning thoughts of her shopping trip. 'Very well, I'll be in as soon as I can,' she replied briefly.

The day proved to be even more hectic than a normal shift for Natalie, and by lunchtime she'd made up her mind that she would have further words with Roger Lomax.

Because of the many road-traffic accidents that morning, resulting in a full emergency surgical list for Theatre, some routine operations had to be postponed. This alone created many problems, but, coupled with severe staff shortages, the backlog of patients would be considerable.

Natalie worked steadily, standing in wherever she was needed in Theatre. Adam was particularly conspicuous by his absence. As Natalie assisted another surgeon, Mr Souter, as he operated on a young women with multiple injuries, including a ruptured spleen, she realised just how used to Adam's methods she had become in the short time she had been at the General.

Once as she was on her way to the canteen to grab a quick cup of tea she encountered Roger Lomax in the corridor that led to the adminstration block.

He looked amazed to see her. 'What are you doing here? I thought you were off duty.'

'I was,' she replied tersely. 'But, thanks to a combination of the weather and staff shortages, I was called in.'

He chose to ignore the implication of her remark, instead saying, 'Have you changed your mind about coming out with me?'

She sighed. 'No, Roger, I haven't.'

'Well, there's no law about us having a sandwich together, is there?' To her consternation, he fell into step beside her.

'Do I gather you've had a frantic day?' he asked a little later as they sat together in the canteen.

'You could say that,' Natalie replied drily. 'But

don't tell me, I know—it isn't your fault and you're only doing your job, just like the rest of us.'

'I wasn't going to say that, actually.' A tinge of amusement entered his eyes. 'What I was going to say was that I've decided to review the situation.'

'Well, thank God for that.' Natalie sighed.

'Don't get too excited; I only said I'd review it— I didn't say I could do anything about it.'

She pulled a face at him. 'How does it feel to have so much power?'

'I wouldn't exactly call it power. An admin's lot is not a happy on.'

'My heart bleeds for you.' She laughed. 'You should try theatre work some time.'

'No, thanks,' he grimaced. 'Seriously, though,' he went on, 'admin's not the cushy number you medics think it is.'

'So why do you do it?'

He shrugged. 'The only thing I'm really any good at is figures, so it seemed logical to do accountancy. When I got bored with that I went on a management course.'

'In Liverpool?'

He nodded.

'And where was it you used to stay when you went to Loch Tummel?'

'Where?' He frowned.

'Loch Tummel,' she repeated, and when his expression remained blank she said, 'You said you spent your holidays at Pitlochry. I wondered whereabouts you stayed in the area.'

'Oh, yes.' He hesitated. 'Um, they were mainly camping holidays. We were usually under canvas. We did a lot of climbing and walking.' He glanced at his watch and she noticed that he suddenly seemed tense, uneasy about something. 'I'm sorry, Natalie,' he said, standing up, 'but would you excuse me for a moment while I make a phone call?'

'Of course.' Idly she watched him as he threaded his way through the crowd in the canteen to the public phone booth in the foyer. She felt a vague sense of disappointment, for she had hoped he would want to talk about Scotland. He had seemed so keen yesterday, but now it was almost as if he'd lost interest.

When he returned to the table he was smiling and somehow he seemed more relaxed. He ordered another drink, and when he sat down again he mentioned her joining the hospital social club.

'I thought it would be a good place to meet people, as I didn't know anyone when I arrived,' she explained.

'Except Adam Curtis.' He said it quietly and so casually that she wasn't sure if she'd heard him correctly.

Carefully she set her cup down in its saucer. 'I'm sorry, what did you say?'

'I said, Adam Curtis. You must have known him. After all, you're living with him, aren't you?'

She stared at him, then took a deep breath. 'I think, Roger, there's something we need to get straight.'

'Really?'

'I am not, as you put it, living with Adam Curtis.'

'But you are living in his house?' His reply was swift.

'I am a guest in his house, and that is a vastly different thing from living with him,' Natalie replied firmly.

He stared at her as if he found it difficult to believe, then he shrugged. 'And how do you come to be a guest of the great man himself? There can't be too many of us humble minions who would qualify for that dubious honour.'

She took a deep breath. 'Not that it's any business of yours or anyone else's, but Adam Curtis and I are related.'

She thought she detected a flicker of interest in his eyes before he said, 'Well, that puts rather a different slant on things.'

'What do you mean?' Immediately she was on the defensive.

'Well, believe it or not, Natalie, but even I was a bit wary about chatting up Adam Curtis's woman, but now you've explained the situation. . .' He trailed off, but Natalie glared angrily at him.

'So how does this make such a big difference?' she asked at last.

Roger sighed and stared at her for a long moment, allowing his gaze to travel over her hair and her features, finally coming to rest on her mouth; then, placing his elbows on the table, he leaned forward. 'I fancy you, Natalie,' he said, bluntly. 'I fancied you from the moment I set eyes on you. As soon as you stood up in that meeting and I caught sight of this glorious red hair,' he reached out and lifted a strand of her hair, 'I said to myself, "I want that woman."'

Natalie felt an involuntary shudder pass through her; then the colour flooded her cheeks. She had the sudden feeling that Roger Lomax was going to be very persistent.

CHAPTER SIX

WITH a sigh Natalie set down her pen and, leaning back in her chair, she stretched. The report she was writing seemed to be going on forever, and she still had some schedules and rotas to finalise before she went off duty. She was pleased, however, that she was due for a couple of days' leave. She had nothing in particular planned, apart from the fact that she had promised Jane Markham she would help Adam look after Timothy while Jane spent the night in hospital.

Adam was due back from Brussels the following day, and Jane was being admitted to the gynae ward during the morning.

It had been a strange week, and Natalie had found that she had missed Adam terribly both at work and at Sheridan House, which had seemed bleak and empty without him. She bitterly regretted that they had parted on a sour note, but that didn't alter the fact that she now knew that Adam had another woman in his life.

Whenever Natalie thought about it she felt a pang of misery, and she longed to ask someone and find out about the relationship. The trouble was that she didn't know who to ask; she was pretty certain that none of the staff knew, because if they did there were sure to have been rumours. She toyed with the idea of asking Jane, but decided against it, as it wasn't really fair to ask Jane to gossip about her employer. With a sigh she put her head down and tried to get her mind back on to her work.

She was just battling with an operating list for the following week and wondering if she could fit in an operation for varicose veins between a double hernia and a bronchoscopy when someone tapped on her office door. Before she had a chance to reply the door opened and Roger Lomax put his head round.

'Ah, here you are,' he said, coming right into the room and shutting the door behind him. 'If I didn't know better I'd have said you've been avoiding me today.'

'Of course I haven't, Roger.' She sighed again. He had been so persistent in the last week that it really was beginning to irritate her. He seemed to have been around wherever she went; in the canteen, the rest-room, or even waiting in the car park when she finished work. 'I've been up to my eyes in paperwork and I've hardly set foot outside this office all day.'

He grinned at her, then perched on the edge of her desk. 'I wanted to ask you if you'd come to the social club tonight. They're having a bit of a bash down there.'

She hesitated, for she had already promised Lyn that she would go with her, but if Roger was going to be there she wondered if she might give it a miss.

Before she could make an excuse, however, he broke into her thoughts.

'Come on!' He spoke persuasively. 'I won't see you at all for the next couple of days.'

'Oh?' she looked up questioningly, trying to keep the relief from her voice.

He shook his head. 'No, I've got to go and visit my old dad. The old boy's getting on, and he looks forward to my visits.'

'Do you have to go all the way to Liverpool?'

'No, he's in an old folks' home in Birmingham.' He shrugged. 'You know how it is. . .'

'Of course,' Natalie smiled. 'Actually, I have a busy couple of days too. You remember I told you about Timothy, Adam's housekeeper's little boy?'

Roger nodded. 'The one who likes modelling?'

She laughed. 'That's the one. Well, his mum has to come into hospital, so I'll probably be helping to keep an eye on him.'

'That settles it. All this "doing good" is reason enough for us to spend this evening together, don't you agree?'

She laughed then and stood up. 'Actually, Roger, you're a bit late with your invitation.'

'What do you mean?' His expression changed and he looked suspicious.

'As it happens, I will be going to the club tonight, but I've already promised Lyn Irving I'll go with her. Isn't it a retirement party for one of the porters?'

He nodded briefly, then frowned. 'Couldn't you make some excuse and say you're coming with me?'

'No, Roger, I couldn't,' she said firmly, then, standing up, she looked down at the mountain of work still on her desk. 'I've had enough of this—I think I'll call it a day.'

'Well, never mind, I'll see you there anyway,' he said, and without waiting for a reply he slid off her desk and with a wink he was gone, closing the door behind him.

For a moment Natalie stared at the closed door. She really didn't know what she was going to do about Roger Lomax. Until now his attentions, although irritating, had been harmless enough, but she had the feeling that he wasn't going to be patient for much longer. She knew the day was coming when she was going to have to be very firm and tell him to leave her alone, but she had a nasty feeling that he would prove difficult when she did that.

He had made it very plain that he found her very attractive and that he wanted a full-scale relationship with her, and, while Natalie didn't mind being friendly with him at work, there was no way she wanted more than that. How could she, feeling the way she did about Adam? But she could hardly tell Roger Lomax that when Adam himself didn't know and wouldn't be interested even if he did, if the company on his last night at Sheridan House had been anything to go by.

She replaced the cap on her pen, collected up her papers and returned them to a folder, then with a last glance round her office she opened the door, switched off the light and stepped out into the corridor.

When she got to Sheridan House she found Timothy waiting for her in the hall.

'Look,' he said solemnly, holding up a model of an owl, 'I made it, in a mould, from wax, just like in the book.'

'It's lovely, Timothy!' Natalie admired the model. 'You're a very clever boy. Is your mum around?'

He nodded. 'She's in the kitchen.'

'I'll just go and have a word with her,' said Natalie.

A feeling of warmth and a delicious aroma greeted her as she pushed open the kitchen door. The warmth was from the large Aga and the aroma from a batch of bread that Jane had just lifted from the oven.

She turned and smiled at Natalie. 'I thought I'd better stock up for the next few days if I'm to be out of action. Mr Curtis does like his home-baked bread.'

'Do you know what time he's due back tomorrow, Jane?' asked Natalie.

'Oh, quite early in the morning, I think. I shall take Timothy to school as usual before going to the hospital. Then Mr Curtis said he would pick him up later.'

'Well, I'm off duty if for any reason he can't,' said Natalie, then added, 'In fact, I was wondering— Timothy finishes school at three doesn't he?' When

Jane nodded she went on, 'Do you think he'd like to go to Madame Tussaud's to see the waxworks? He seems so interested in wax models since he had that book.'

'I'm sure he would.' Jane straightened up from the Aga. 'But why don't you ask him?' She nodded towards the door, and when Natalie turned she found Timothy had come into the room.

'How about it, Timothy?' she asked. 'I was just asking your mum if you'd like to go to Madame Tussaud's tomorrow after school. Do you know what that is?'

His eyes shone. 'Yes,' he said excitedly, 'it's a brill place—Miss Winters told us all about it. They used to chop people's heads off, then make wax models of them. D'you think we'll see that?' he asked solemnly.

'I hope not, Timothy,' Natalie laughed.

'What about Mr Curtis?' he asked suddenly.

'What about him?'

'Well, he said he would meet me from school. . .' He looked worried, then, his expression brightening, he said, 'I know—he could come with us, couldn't he?'

'Well,. . .he may not want to,' said Natalie dubiously.

'Oh, I 'spect he will,' said Timothy. 'Mr Curtis is ace.'

'Well, that's settled, then,' said Natalie firmly. 'If Mr Curtis wants to come to the waxworks with us he's very welcome.'

'It's awfully good of you,' said Jane as Timothy disappeared to his room. 'I really don't know what I'd have done. . .'

'It's nothing, really. Besides, I shall enjoy a trip to the waxworks.' Natalie smiled. 'I believe all newcomers to London go there, don't they?'

Jane laughed and nodded. 'I believe so. It's only us Londoners who don't go to these places.' Then she grew serious, a worried expression crossing her face. 'I shall be glad when the next couple of days are over,' she confided.

'Don't worry, everything will be all right.' Natalie reached out and reassuringly touched her arm.

'I feel so alone when anything like this happens,' said Jane quietly as she slid the freshly baked loaves from the trays on to the table.

'Don't you have any family?'

'No, not now; there's just Timmy and me. I suppose it was partly my fault, but I lost touch with my family when I had Timothy and I haven't bothered since.'

'Perhaps you should,' said Natalie gently.

'Yes, maybe I should.' Jane paused reflectively, then briskly changed the subject. 'Will you be in for dinner this evening, Natalie?'

'Yes, I'll be here for dinner, but I shall be going out later to a party at the hospital social club,' she replied.

The club had taken on a festive air when Natalie and Lyn arrived that evening. The bar was open, there was a running buffet, and a mobile disco, complete with strobe lighting, had been set up in one corner.

'This looks like fun,' said Lyn, peering round the rather dim interior of the club. 'But there aren't many here yet—either that or we're early.

'Which one of the porters is retiring?' asked Natalie, who hadn't had a chance to get to know all the staff in the short time she had been at the General.

'Len Drake,' explained Lyn. 'He was deputy head porter, so quite a few of the big brass should be here.' She glanced up sharply as a figure detached himself from a group at the bar and began walking towards them. 'See what I mean?' she muttered out of the side of her mouth. 'Even Casanova Lomax is here.'

Natalie giggled. 'What did you call him?'

'Casanova. . .didn't you know? Fancies himself as a right ladies' man. I hear he's been hanging around you. . .' murmured Lyn, then, looking up, she said, 'Hello, Mr Lomax. Slumming tonight, are we? Didn't expect to see you here.'

'Good evening, ladies. Of course I should be here. Len Drake is a very popular man.' Briefly he allowed his gaze to flicker over Natalie. 'Now what can I get you to drink?'

While Roger went off to the bar to order drinks Lyn threw Natalie a quizzical glance. 'So tell me, is there any truth in those rumours I heard. Are you and he. . .?'

'Certainly not—just friends,' replied Natalie firmly.

'I've heard that one before.' Lyn frowned and seemed about to say more, then she appeared to change her mind and instead she said, 'I was beginning to think something was happening between you and Adam Curtis.'

Natalie started. 'Whatever gave you that idea?'

'Oh, I don't know—various things. . .the way he looks at you, for a start.'

'Well, you're mistaken, I can assure you.' Natalie laughed then and added, 'I've been down that road once before, you see.'

'Whatever do you mean?' Lyn was obviously curious and wasn't going to let go until Natalie explained.

'It was when I was at school and I first met Adam. My brother brought him home and I thought he was the best thing since sliced bread; then my glamorous cousin came on the scene, and even if I'd stood on my head and done cartwheels he wouldn't have noticed me.'

'That was then; what about now?'

Natalie frowned. 'Now?'

'Yes,' said Lyn with a grin. 'Do you still think he's the best thing since sliced bread?'

'Oh, I've grown up now,' replied Natalie evasively, then turned to take her drink from Roger.

When Lyn's attention was gradually taken elsewhere Roger guided Natalie towards a table on the

far side of the club, away from the crowd around
the bar.

'You know something?' he said a little later as
they sipped their drinks. 'You look sensational
tonight.'

'Do I?' Natalie looked a little startled at the
intensity behind his remark, but she wasn't dis-
pleased. She had chosen to wear a cream skirt in a
soft jersey material with a matching long-line jacket
and a camisole top in a dark chocolate colour.

'Have you thought any more about looking for a
flat?' he asked, and there was the same intense note
in his voice.

She shrugged. 'Well, yes, I have, of course. I
can't impose on Adam forever.'

'I was wondering if you'd like me to help you find
somewhere?'

'That's kind of you, Roger,' she replied, 'but I'm
sure I can manage.' The last thing she wanted was
for Roger to be involved when she looked for other
accommodation.

As the evening progressed more and more people
began to arrive. To Natalie's dismay, Lyn seemed
to be otherwise engaged with a certain ambulance
driver, leaving her stuck with Roger.

As Roger had said, Len Drake was a popular
member of the portering team, and by the time
Harry Jones, the portering manager, stood up to
make the presentations it seemed that every depart-
ment in the hospital was represented.

'Harry's like a general with those men,' mur-

mured Roger in Natalie's ear as Harry sat down and
Len took his place to make his thank-you speech.
'The porters are like his own private army.'

'You mean like the Duke of Atholl?' Natalie
whispered.

'Who?' Roger turned and frowned at her as if he
didn't have a clue what she was talking about.

'The Duke of Atholl—you know,' she replied.

He still didn't answer, but later, when the
speeches were over, the disco was under way and
couples were drifting on to the floor, he pulled her
up and guided her on to the small dance-floor.

He held her close as they swayed to the music—
too close, she thought uneasily as his hands roamed
down her back and over her hips. She squirmed and
tried to wriggle out of his grasp, but he only laughed
and held her tighter, pressing his hard body against
hers. He began to breathe heavily, and as she
realised the effect she was having on him she
decided to suggest that they sit down, but before he
could say anything Roger spoke.

'So who is this duke you were talking about just
now?' he asked.

She leaned back a little so she could see his
expression. 'The Duke of Atholl,' she answered.

'Yes, I know—you said that,' he gave a husky
laugh and ran his hands down her thighs, 'but who
is he exactly, and what has he got to do with Harry
Jones?'

She gave a little laugh of exasperation. 'You said
Harry Jones ran the porters as if they were his own

private army, and it made me think of the Duke of Atholl, because he's the only person in Britain who has a private army.'

'Is that a fact?' he grinned. 'Sorry, but I've never heard of him. Obviously my education wasn't as good as yours.'

'It's nothing to do with my education—he was a neighbour!' Natalie laughed. 'He owns Blair Castle.' She grew serious again. 'But I thought you would have known that, Roger. Anyone who goes to Pitlochry visits Blair Castle—don't tell me you didn't?'

He shook his head.

She was silent for a while, relieved that his hands were now harmlessly around her waist. They continued dancing, then, when his hands became adventurous again in a bid to divert him she said 'You know something Roger, I don't think you know as much about Scotland as you led me to believe.'

He shrugged, pulling a face. 'Don't know what you mean—marvellous place.'

'So just how many times have you visited Pitlochry?' she asked suspiciously.

'Oh, holidays, you know, that sort of thing.' His reply was evasive and he appeared to be looking around the club as he spoke.

Natalie noticed that his eyes had suddenly narrowed, but this time she was determined not to let the matter drop. 'How many holidays?' she persisted.

'One or two. . .'

'One? Or two?'

'Well, one, actually.'

'And when exactly was that?'

'Let's see, now; I think I was about eleven at the time.'

She stared at him, shocked, then when he grinned she was forced in spite of her exasperation to smile at his audacity. 'So why did you. . .?'

'Why did I pretend I knew the place so well?' He looked at her as if he wanted to devour her, and as he spoke he tightened his grip, drawing her even closer. 'I'll tell you why, Natalie my love; it was because I saw it as the only way I could get to know you quickly. You're obviously proud of Scotland and were missing your home. I figured if I pretended I knew all about it you would want to talk.'

'Well. . .of all the devious. . .' She was speechless, but found herself laughing up at him.

He too laughed, then, lowering his head, he nuzzled the side of her neck.

It was then, as she attempted to pull away from him, deciding he had gone far enough, that she had the unmistakable feeling that she was being watched.

She looked up, and over Roger's shoulder she saw someone standing by the bar. He was beyond the circle of lights and for a moment she couldn't distinguish his face. Then with a jolt she realised it was Adam.

CHAPTER SEVEN

'OH!'NATALIE said. 'There's Adam.'

Roger lifted his head. 'Who?' he said in an uninterested tone.

'Adam; Adam Curtis,' she repeated.

'Oh, him; yes, I know. I saw him some while ago when he first came in.'

'Why didn't you say?' She pulled away from him as she spoke and began walking across the floor towards Adam.

'I didn't know I had to,' Roger muttered as he followed her.

As they approached Natalie could see there was a strange expression on Adam's face, a cross between a scowl and a look of suspicion.

'Hello, Adam,' she said, suddenly conscious that he must have been watching Roger and herself and that for some reason her heart was thumping wildly. 'I didn't think you were coming home until tomorrow.'

'I wasn't,' he replied, and his tone was flat, 'but I changed my mind. It looks as if it's a good job I did, otherwise they'd have been without a general surgeon tomorrow morning. The rota was impossible to start with——' he glared at Roger as he spoke as if he held him directly responsible for the staff shortages '—and now,' he continued, his tone icy, 'both Peter Farmer and Uri Adahbi have gone down with this wretched flu. I suggest,' he carried on, staring directly at Roger now, 'that you come along to Theatre tomorrow and see the situation for yourself.'

'I'm off duty for a couple of days——' began Roger.

'And so was I supposed to be!' replied Adam through gritted teeth.

Natalie threw him an apprehensive glance and noticed a vein that stood out at the side of his neck. She couldn't remember ever seeing him so angry, but she had an uneasy feeling that his anger wasn't only to do with staff shortages.

'I'll take you up on your offer when I get back,' Roger continued as if Adam hadn't interrupted, then, turning, he said, 'Can I get you another drink, Natalie?'

'No, thank you, Roger; in fact, I was just thinking it's time I was getting home,' she replied.

'Right, I'll run you back,' he said.

'There won't be any need for that,' Adam intervened. 'I'm going home now. Natalie can come with me.'

Natalie stiffened, suddenly aware of the heightened tension between the two men. 'I'll get my coat,' she said, then fled to the ladies' cloakroom. In the privacy of the small powder-room she splashed cold water on her burning face, then stared at her reflection in the mirror. Whatever was Adam doing in the club, and why had he come home early from Brussels? He had seemed angry to find her with Roger, but why should it matter to him? Roger, on the other hand, seemed to be deliberately trying to provoke Adam. With a silent groan she dried her face, then applied fresh lipstick and combed her hair.

When she returned to the club she could see Adam waiting for her in the foyer while Roger was leaning against the bar.

'Goodbye, Roger,' she said as she fastened her coat.

He grimaced, then shrugged.

'I'll see you in a couple of days,' she added. 'I hope you find your father well.'

He sighed. Then, glancing up through the open doors to the foyer beyond, he said, 'You'd better not keep the great man waiting.'

There was a decided note of sarcasm in his voice, and Natalie frowned, but he had turned back to the bar.

She hesitated for a moment then, turning sharply, she hurried from the club. As she passed Lyn Irving she was vaguely conscious of her friend's worried frown, but she didn't stop.

'Are you ready?' Adam raised one eyebrow as he turned from a notice board which he appeared to have been studying intently. Natalie, however, had the distinct impression that if he'd been asked he wouldn't have had a clue what was on the board.

'Yes,' she replied shortly, 'I'm ready.' Suddenly

she felt sorry for Roger Lomax and for one unreasonable moment she felt annoyed with Adam.

Then as he held open the door of his Daimler and she slid into the passenger-seat she dismissed her annoyance. After all, it was good of him to offer to take her home, and it was probably a blessing in disguise, as she might have been forced to fight Roger off, if his behaviour on the dance-floor had been an indication of what was to follow.

They pulled out into the sparse, late-night traffic, and Natalie rested her head against the soft leather seat. It was a damp night, with a fine drizzle that soon required Adam to switch on the windscreen-wipers.

They were silent at first, then unexpectedly Adam spoke. Keeping his eyes on the road, he said, 'Were you having trouble back there?'

'Trouble?' She threw him a sideways glance but could only see the outline of his profile in the darkness.

'Yes, with Lomax.'

'No, not really. Why?'

'I thought he appeared to be acting in a most objectionable way.'

She stiffened. There was something in his tone that she found irritating. 'No, everything was fine,' she said firmly.

He was silent again, then he said tightly, 'You mean you welcome that sort of thing?'

'What sort of thing?' She was aware that her voice had risen slightly.

'Being pawed in public by a man like that.'

'I was not being pawed, as you put it. We were merely dancing and having a laugh because. . .' She trailed off, uncertain if she could explain what they had been laughing at.

Adam, however, was not to be put off. 'Because of what?' he asked shortly.

She sighed and, taking a deep breath, said, 'Because when I first met him he told me he knew Pitlochry very well, having spent all his holidays there. Now it turns out that he only spent one holiday there, and that was when he was eleven years old.'

'So he lied to you.'

'Well. . .not exactly——'

'And you found that fact amusing?'

'The point was that he used the connection to try to get to know me. I don't really see it as lying.'

Adam didn't reply immediately, and Natalie bit her lip and stared out of the car at the lighted shop windows. She really didn't see what it had to do with Adam whether Roger had lied to her or not, and she had just made up her mind to tell him so when he said abruptly, 'So have you seen him very much in the past week?'

She shrugged.

'Well?' It was almost as if he was demanding an answer, and he took his eyes briefly from the road and glared at her.

'Well what?' she asked indignantly.

'Have you been seeing him?'

'I've seen him at work, naturally.'

'That isn't what I meant.'

'Then just what do you mean, Adam?' Angrily she stared at him.

'Do you find him attractive?'

'He's amusing.'

'Amusing. So is that reason enough for you to be going out with him?'

'Who said I was going out with him? I didn't say I was, but even if I am I can't see why you should be so concerned. I'm not a child and I'm perfectly capable of taking care of myself.'

He didn't answer, and as they pulled up outside Sheridan House she flung him a sharp glance, but his face was in shadow and she couldn't see his expression. He turned off the ignition and they sat in silence in the darkness. In the end it was Natalie who broke the silence.

'Tell me, Adam,' she said, 'what is it exactly that you have against Roger Lomax?'

She sensed him grip the steering-wheel tightly while he took a deep breath as if to calm his temper.

'I don't trust the man,' he said abruptly. 'I don't like his type, and I don't think he's the right type for you.'

She stared at him, uncertain whether to be angry or to laugh. 'I'm still not certain what you think gives you the right to vet who I do or don't go out with.' When he didn't reply she said, 'I can't believe you're taking your responsibilities that far just because I'm staying in your house and because we're distantly related by marriage.'

He shifted restlessly in his seat, and when he still didn't answer she went on, 'Oh, I know you said you promised James, and all that rubbish, but isn't this rather taking things to extremes?'

'I'm sorry, Natalie,' he said quietly, 'but I still happen to think Lomax is a nasty piece of work and not your type.'

She stared at his profile, slightly exasperated by this unexpected streak of stubbornness in him and wishing that his concern for her was born of jealousy, but knowing that was highly unlikely after having seen him with his glamorous girlfriend.

'So what sort of man would you say was my type?' she asked impulsively.

'What?' He turned sharply, catching his breath as he stared at her in the darkness. Then in a totally unexpected movement he reached out and pulled her roughly towards him, his strong hands circling her face, his fingers becoming entangled in her hair, and before she had time to think what was happening his mouth had covered hers.

His kiss was hard and demanding, and at first, because he had startled her, she resisted and fought against him, trying to push him away.

Then gradually, as the ferocity went out of his kiss, to be replaced by sheer desire, she realised this was the moment she'd waited so long for, and she found herself responding, her lips parting beneath his, welcoming the questing of his teeth and tongue.

Then, as abruptly as it had started, it was over and he thrust her away.

'I know what sort of man would be your type,' he muttered. 'And Lomax could never satisfy you.'

Natalie sat quite still as she tried to collect her chaotic thoughts. Adam had turned his face away from her and was leaning on the steering-wheel as if he too was trying to recover.

He remained silent, and at last she opened the car door and stepped out on to the wet road, and when he did nothing to stop her she hurried indoors, not stopping until she reached the privacy of her room.

As she shut her bedroom door and leaned against it she realised she was shaking. Could Adam have realised how close he'd been to the truth when he'd kissed her, in some way implying that what she needed was a man like him? If only he knew he was the one man she had wanted for as long as she could remember, first as her teenage fantasy, but now, having found him again as a woman, wanting him with an intensity that had shaken her to the very core.

If only she could tell him how she felt, that Roger Lomax meant nothing to her, that he, Adam, had simply goaded her into answering his questions in the way she had.

His kiss had been everything she had ever dreamed it would be, awakening hidden desires deep within her, leaving her emotions taut and screaming for more.

But he was still as much a mystery to her as he
had ever been. James had hinted that he had never
got over Suzanne, and at the time Natalie had
imagined that to mean that he had had no other
relationships since her death, but the presence of
the blonde woman had exploded that theory, leaving Natalie no closer to knowing Adam's thoughts.

There had been moments when she had thought
he was interested in her—during their evening at
the theatre, afterwards when he had stopped her
briefly on the stairs and then when they had dined
together—but something had always happened
afterwards to make her change her opinion.

When finally she went to sleep her dreams were
troubled and haunted by a figure in theatre greens
complete with mask. In the dream she believed the
man to be Adam, but when he removed his mask
and attempted to make love to her she saw it was
Roger Lomax.

The following morning when Natalie came downstairs she was relieved to find that Adam had already
left for the hospital. She wasn't sure how she was
going to face him after the scene in his car the
previous evening.

All thoughts of that were soon put out of her
mind, however, when she found Jane in a highly
anxious state, not so much about her forthcoming
operation but over leaving Timothy.

'You mustn't worry about him,' said Natalie
firmly as she helped herself to orange juice from the
fridge.

'No, Mum,' said Timothy, looking up from his bowl of Rice Crispies, 'you mustn't worry. I'll be all right.' He looked at Natalie. 'I told Mr Curtis about the waxworks,' he said.

'Did you? And what did he say?' She found herself holding her breath as she waited to see what Adam's reply had been.

'He said he was working this morning but if he was finished he'd come with us. But he said he'd play draughts with me tonight whatever. Is he going to do your operation, Mum?'

Jane shook her head. 'No, he isn't. Now, Timmy, you must promise me that you won't be a nuisance to Natalie or to Mr Curtis—it's very good of them both to give up their free time to look after you.'

'Of course I won't.' He looked quite disgusted at the idea, and Natalie smiled.

'How were you intending getting to the hospital?' she asked Jane.

'On the bus. I thought I'd take Timothy to school then just carry on the next few stops to the hospital.'

'I've got a better idea. You and Timothy get yourselves ready, I'll have a cup of coffee, then I'll take you both in the car. How's that?'

'Well. . .it's very kind of you, but——'

'No buts—I insist,' said Natalie firmly as she saw Jane's dubious look.

'Very well. Thank you,' replied Jane gratefully as she hustled Timothy off to clean his teeth and get his school bag.

Natalie poured a coffee and, curling her hands

around the mug, sat at the big kitchen table, glad of
a quiet moment's respite. She'd had a bad night
after the strange events of the evening, finding sleep
almost impossible as she'd tried to make sense of
what had happened.

She became so lost in her thoughts again that she
hadn't realised that Jane and Timothy had come
back into the kitchen and were waiting for her.

They dropped Timothy off at his school, with
Natalie promising that she would be there at three
o'clock to meet him; then they proceeded to the
hospital.

'I hope I didn't make a blunder last night,' said
Jane suddenly as Natalie drew up at a set of traffic-
lights.

'In what way?'

Jane glanced quickly at her. 'Well, when Mr
Curtis arrived home unexpectedly from Brussels he
asked me where you were.'

'Did he?' Natalie stiffened slightly. 'And what did
you say?'

'I told him that you'd gone to a party at the
hospital social club.'

Natalie jumped as Jane nudged her and nodded
at the lights, which had changed to green while they
had been talking. The car behind sounded its horn
and she pulled away.

'I'm sorry if I did wrong,' said Jane.

'What makes you think you did wrong?'

'I don't know,' Jane hesitated. 'It's just that Mr
Curtis seemed angry, and that's not like him.'

'No, it isn't,' murmured Natalie cryptically, then she frowned. 'Was there a phone call for him from the hospital?'

Jane shook her head. 'No, but there wouldn't have been, would there? He wasn't expected back until today.'

'That's right,' agreed Natalie, then fell silent, wondering just why Adam had come to the hospital last night. She had imagined that it had been something to do with the staff shortages and his having to operate that morning. Now she wasn't so sure. Suddenly she was aware that Jane was still looking anxiously at her. 'It's all right, Jane,' she said, 'please don't worry. Everything was OK.'

Jane gave a sigh of relief. 'Thank goodness for that. I was really worried that I'd put my foot in it.' She glanced up as the hospital buildings loomed into sight. 'Oh, we're here. I'll be glad when this is over.'

Natalie parked in the car park outside the large obstetric and gynaecological wing, and as Jane got out of the car she locked the doors and took Jane's case from the boot.

'Thank you so much for bringing me,' said Jane as she took her case.

'It's all right, I'm coming in with you.'

'Are you?' Jane's eyes widened. 'You don't have to. . .'

'Oh yes, I do,' said Natalie firmly. 'I can't think of anything worse than being admitted to a hospital ward on your own.'

It seemed strange to Natalie to be seeing things

from the patient's angle when they arrived in the gynae ward. They were greeted by the staff nurse in charge, who handed them over to an enrolled nurse. Natalie waited while the nurse took Jane to her bed and took her particulars, admitting her to the ward, then slipped back to see her for a couple of minutes.

Dressed in a pink nightie and without her glasses, Jane was sitting up in bed, looking rather apprehensive. 'I'm having the op at two o'clock,' she explained. 'I suppose that's why I wasn't allowed any breakfast.'

Natalie nodded. 'Have you everything you need?'

'Yes, I think so.' Jane looked around. 'I won't be here long enough to need much, thank goodness.'

'Well, if you're comfortable, I'll be going,' replied Natalie.

'Of course, I'm taking up quite enough of your day off as it is. You'll be wanting to get home.'

'Actually I'm going to pop down to the theatre for a while to see how things are going. They're so short-staffed at the moment.'

After saying goodbye to Jane, telling her not to worry about Timmy, and that she would come and pick her up the following day, Natalie slipped out of the gynae wing and down to the theatre unit.

The first person she saw was Lyn Irving, who was working in the office. She looked up in surprise as Natalie entered.

'My word, can't anyone stay away from this place? First Mr Curtis, then Jon Bell, now you, and you're all supposed to be off duty.'

'I had to bring a friend in to gynae,' explained Natalie. 'I thought I'd just see how things are going.'

'Well, we're coping. . .or rather we were, until Medical sent down an emergency.' Lyn nodded towards theatre one. 'Mr Curtis has just started operating, but they're one short in there.'

'Well, it's a good job I came, then, isn't it?' Natalie was already taking off her coat.

'Natalie,' said Lyn as she would have gone into her office, 'was everything all right last night?'

'Of course.' Natalie attempted a bright smile. 'Why do you ask?'

'I don't know. . .' Lyn hesitated. 'It was just that Mr Curtis was looking like a thunder-cloud, and Roger Lomax—well, I'm really not sure about him. . .'

'It was all right, Lyn honestly,' said Natalie, hoping she sounded more convincing than she was feeling. 'I'm sorry I went home a bit suddenly, but Adam offered me a lift.'

'Oh, I wasn't worried about that,' said Lyn. With a grin she said, 'As it happened, I had a lift home myself,' then, growing more serious again, she added, 'I just thought there might have been some trouble.'

'No, nothing like that,' replied Natalie as she made her escape.

Fifteen minutes later she was scrubbed up, wearing her greens, her white clogs, mask, and with her hair tucked away beneath a surgical cap, and quietly, with the minimum of fuss, she slipped into the theatre where Adam was operating.

Jon Bell looked up and nodded to her from his seat at the patient's head, and she received a grateful murmur from one of the nursing team, but Adam appeared to be concentrating deeply on what he was doing and it was some time before he looked up.

Then, as he straightened, their eyes met briefly above their masks and her heart started doing crazy things.

But the expression in his dark eyes showed no surprise. Instead it implied that he had known she would be there.

CHAPTER EIGHT

'THERE really isn't anything more we can do,' said Adam quietly as the patient was wheeled away into the recovery-room.

'What's his history?' asked Natalie, aware of Adam's frustration, knowing how much he hated to be forced to admit defeat.

'He was admitted as an emergency with acute abdominal pain, vomiting and a rigid abdomen. The original diagnosis was peritonitis, then almost as soon as I started operating I could see we had more on our hands than that. The primary tumour appeared to be in the colon, but there were extensive secondaries in the liver.'

'How old is he?' asked Natalie, and glanced at the case file.

'Sixty-eight.' Adam shook his head. 'I've resectioned the tumour in the colon and all that can be done now is to make him as comfortable as possible and control the pain. Would you phone Surgical, please, Sister Fraser, and tell the ward sister that I'll speak to the patient's wife?'

Natalie nodded and went to her office to make the call. As she replaced the receiver Adam appeared in the doorway. 'Did Jane get in all right?' he asked.

'Yes, I brought her in after we'd dropped Timothy off at school.'

'That was good of you—thanks. I'm hoping to get through here by lunchtime so that I can join you for the waxworks trip.'

'Don't worry if you can't—I'll take him.'

'He seemed keen for me to go as well, but if you'd rather I didn't. . .' An edge had crept into Adam's voice.

'Of course not; that isn't what I meant at all.' Natalie was suddenly aware that the colour had flooded her face, and for a moment they simply stared at each other. The tension between them was almost electric, then, as her eyes came to rest on his mouth and she was reminded that only hours before those lips had claimed hers, she drew in her breath sharply.

'Natalie. . . I. . .' he began haltingly, then he was abruptly interrupted by the ringing of the telephone on the desk between them, and as she answered it she was left wondering what it was he had been going to say.

'It's another emergency,' she said in reply to his raised eyebrows as she hung up. 'An eleven-year-old girl with acute appendicitis.'

They worked steadily for the rest of the morning, then at midday Adam's place was taken by a locum consultant surgeon and Natalie's by the sister on late shift.

'I think that leaves us with a clear conscience to grab a bite of lunch,' said Adam as he fell into step beside Natalie as she left the theatre unit. He glanced at his watch. 'I think it had better be the canteen if we're to collect young Timothy from his school, don't you?'

She agreed, and moments later after they had selected soup, hot rolls and salad from the self-service bar they carried them to the window-table, where they sat down.

'It strikes me that it was a good job we came in,' said Adam as he buttered a bread roll.

She nodded in agreement, then casually asked, 'How did you know the unit was so short-staffed today?'

'My secretary told me.' He answered without hesitation.

Natalie nodded. Of course, she thought, that was how he'd known. 'I suppose Miss Rolf was in touch with you while you were in Brussels?'

He frowned and shook his head. 'No, as a matter of fact she wasn't.' He hesitated, then said, 'I saw her last night.'

'Last night?'

'Yes, when I came to the hospital. I saw her then and she told me how desperate the situation was.'

'Ah, I see.' Natalie thoughtfully sipped her vegetable soup. So that was how he'd known. But it didn't explain why he'd come to the hospital in the first place. He could, of course, simply have gone there to collect papers or something from his office, but that still didn't explain his presence in the social club. The more Natalie thought about it the more convinced she became that his being there had something to do with the fact that Jane had told him that she, Natalie, had gone there.

As she thought of the social club her thoughts automatically turned to Roger, and once more she found herself feeling sorry for him. She knew she had found his attentions irritating, but it wasn't his fault that she didn't find him attractive, and he had certainly made her laugh at a time when she had been feeling homesick and decidedly hopeless over the situation with Adam.

As they finished their lunch she made up her mind that when he got back from his trip to Birmingham she would apologise for having abandoned him the night before, especially after he'd bought drinks for her.

Adam hadn't made any reference to the previous evening, and for that fact alone she was glad; she certainly didn't want another argument about Roger Lomax, especially as they were spending the rest of the day with Timothy.

They travelled to Timothy's school in Adam's Daimler, having left Natalie's car in the hospital car park.

'We'll pick your car up later,' he said as he negotiated the busy afternoon traffic.

She nodded. 'I was thinking that; then I could call in and see Jane at the same time.'

'And I'll take Timothy home and start the evening meal,' replied Adam solemnly.

Natalie smiled. 'You sound like an old married man.'

As soon as she'd said it she could have bitten out her tongue. But before she had the chance to say anything by way of atonement Adam said quietly, 'Aren't you forgetting? I was one once.'

She threw him a glance, half fearful, half curious, for there had been a strange edge to his voice.

'I'm sorry, Adam. That was thoughtless of me,' she said.

They were silent for a while, and she turned her head to look out of the car window at the bleak wintry day. They were nearly into March now, but there was no sign of any improvement in the weather.

'It was Adam who broke the silence. 'Really,' he said, 'it should be me apologising to you, not the other way round.'

'Why?' She turned to him, her eyes widening.

'My behaviour last night was quite appalling.'

She sighed. 'There's no need to apologise, Adam. I do understand that you have my best interests at heart, but there really isn't any need to worry about Roger Lomax. I wasn't too sure about him myself at first, but now I'm pretty certain he's quite harmless. I think he might have been a bit put out last night, but I'll explain when I see him again and I'm sure he'll understand.'

'I wasn't apologising for upsetting Lomax,' said Adam tersely.

'Oh. . .oh, I thought. . .'

'I was apologising for attacking you in the car.'

'Oh, that. . .oh, I see. . .' She lapsed into an embarrassed silence.

The silence dragged on, then, as he brought the big car to a halt before the gates of Timothy's school, he turned to look at her. 'So, am I forgiven for that as well?'

'Yes, of course you are.' She paused and glanced at him. 'I'm not sure why you did it. . .'

He shook his head. 'Neither am I.' Briefly he allowed his eyes to meet hers.

'Maybe,' she said, then hesitated, uncertain whether or not to continue with what she had been going to say, then when Adam raised his eyebrows, obviously waiting for her to continue, she faltered, 'maybe. . . I remind you of Suzanne. . .?'

Almost before she had uttered the words she was aware that his whole body had stiffened, and she found herself holding her breath. At that precise moment Timothy appeared at the gates, accompanied by a young woman who Natalie guessed was his form teacher. He peered anxiously up and down the road, then when he caught sight of Adam's car he said something to the woman, pointed at the car and waved excitedly.

Adam opened the door and said, 'I suppose I'd better identify myself, in case they think we're about to kidnap him.'

After he'd climbed out of the car he slammed the door, then, bending down, he spoke through the partly open window. 'And the answer to your question is no.' He said it abruptly, then added, 'You're nothing like Suzanne, nothing at all.'

Minutes later he opened the rear door and the excited little boy scrambled in, and Natalie realised it was practically the first time she had heard Adam mention Suzanne's name since she had been in London. And what he had said had confirmed what she had once suspected; that no one could ever match up to the beautiful Suzanne or take her place in Adam's heart.

She felt a stab of misery at the prospect, then found herself wondering about the woman she had seen Adam with before he went to Brussels and just where she fitted into the picture, but she had no time for further speculation then, as Timothy claimed her attention.

'Have you seen my mum?' he asked as Adam pulled away from the kerb.'

'I took her into the hospital,' explained Natalie, 'and when I left she was tucked up in bed. I shall call in and see her again later.'

'Will she be able to come home?' he asked eagerly, leaning forward between the front seats of the car.

'Not today,' said Natalie patiently. 'But tomorrow, if the doctor says she can.'

'Are we going to the waxworks now?'

'Yes, Timothy.' It was Adam who answered this time. 'Have you been looking forward to it?'

'Yes. I told the others in my class, and they were dead jealous,' replied Timothy with obvious satisfaction at having been the centre of so much attention.

Half an hour later they joined the queue of tourists in Marylebone Road at the entrance to the famous waxworks, then once inside they watched in amusement as Timothy's entrancement grew with every figure and tableau they saw.

They moved slowly through the Hall of Fame, inspecting models of the royal family, heads of state and public figures, moving on to sports personalities and pop stars. But the figure that seemed to intrigue Timothy the most was that of a teenage girl on one of the landings which at first sight he had believed to be real. It was while he had gone back for a third look that Adam said, 'I'm glad we brought him; it was a marvellous idea of yours.'

'He certainly appears to be enjoying himself,' agreed Natalie with a smile. She had relaxed while they had been inspecting the wax models, and it had felt for all the world as if she, Adam and Timothy were like any one of the other family groups. It was a pleasant feeling, and she found she had forgotten all her recent problems. Adam too seemed happy and relaxed; he had changed before he had left the hospital and he looked casual in dark green cords, a cream sweater and a tan leather jacket.

'He can't convince himself that that girl is made of wax.' Adam leaned back against a banister rail and nodded in amusement towards Timothy, who was staring up into the girl's face in studied concentration. He glanced at his brochure as he spoke. 'It's the Chamber of Horrors next,' he commented.

'Do you think we should take Timmy in there?' asked Natalie doubtfully.

'Of course. All children like to be frightened, don't they? Think of all those fairy stories by the brothers Grimm and co—I've never known a more terrifying collection than that, apart from nursery rhymes, and kids have loved them for centuries.'

Natalie shrugged. 'Well, if you say so—you're the doctor.'

Far from being terrified by the collection of murderers and the instruments of torture in the Chamber of Horrors, Timothy seemed to love every minute of it, and never stopped asking questions.

Some of the other children who were in the Chamber at the same time seemed less enthusiastic, however, and one little girl in particular appeared quite distressed. She clung to her mother's arm, averting her eyes from the monstrous sights in the dimly lit dungeons and hiding her face in the woman's coat. At the same time she asked repeatedly if they could go.

Natalie smiled sympathetically at the mother, a plump, pretty woman with curly dark hair, and the woman shrugged helplessly and nodded towards her other daughter. This girl, somewhat older than her sister, had gone on ahead with a man who Natalie assumed was her father, and she appeared to be enjoying everything she saw, exclaiming and pointing and clutching at her father's arm. They had stopped and were looking at a tableau of Victorian murderers, and as Natalie, Adam and Timothy passed them Natalie heard the girl say, 'But Daddy, why was he called Jack the Ripper?'

'I don't know, love—maybe he ripped his victims' clothes,' the man replied tactfully, and there was something about the slightly cryptic note of amusement in his voice that made Natalie glance at him. He in turn, obviously sensing her interest, looked around, and she found herself staring into the face of Roger Lomax.

There might have been the briefest flicker in those curious yellow-green eyes, then, with no further sign of recognition, he turned away to speak to the child again.

In bewilderment Natalie followed Adam and Timothy out of the dank, almost evil atmosphere of the Chamber of Horrors. Outside Adam turned to wait for her, but if he had seen Roger Lomax he gave no indication that anything untoward had happened.

By the time they left the waxworks and stepped outside into the chill of the late afternoon and to the familiar roar of the London traffic, Natalie was beginning to wonder if the incident had been a figment of her imagination brought about by the unreality of that evil environment.

But later, as they wound they way through the rush-hour traffic in Adam's Daimler, with Timothy in the back eagerly examining the souvenirs and brochures that Adam had bought for him, she leaned her head back on the soft leather upholstery and had time to think. It was then that she knew without a shadow of doubt that what she had seen had been very real. And the more she thought about it the more it seemed to fit.

She had never asked Roger if he was married, she had just assumed that he wasn't, especially when he had made it so plain that he wanted her to go out with him—and that had been real enough, of that she was quite certain; he had not taken any pains to hide his desires—or maybe lust would be a better word, she thought grimly.

Funnily enough, her first reaction as she had followed Adam out of the Chamber had been surprise—surprise that Roger had been there when he should have been in Birmingham, visiting his father. It was only after she had time to think that she realised that too, of course, had been a lie. He probably didn't have a father alive, let alone living in a residential home in Birmingham.

Suddenly she felt angry. How dared he try to chat her up when all the time he was married with a young family? Even the bit about his holidays in Pitlochry had been a lie—Adam had pointed that out, but she had laughed at the time, preferring to believe it had been done with the best of intentions. Now she found herself wondering just how practised a liar Roger Lomax actually was.

Did he make a habit of chatting up the female staff wherever he happened to be working? And if they proved willing, just how far did he allow the charade to go? She shuddered, realising how lucky she'd been that she hadn't been attracted to him—how many others had fallen victim to his persuasive ways? Suddenly she jumped as she realised with a start that Adam had been talking to her and she hadn't heard a word he'd been saying.

'I'm sorry,' she said, shaking her head slightly as if to clear her mind of disturbing images. 'What did you say?'

'I simply asked if you wanted to go straight to the hospital.' He threw her a sharp look, taking his eyes briefly from the road. 'But you were miles away.'

'I know,' she replied abruptly. 'I'm sorry. Yes, Adam, I will go to the hospital. I want to see Jane, then I can pick up my car.'

'Can I see my mum?' said Timothy suddenly from the back seat.

Natalie hesitated, and it was Adam who answered. 'Not just now, old man. Your mother will be very tired at the moment. Natalie will just make sure she's all right. I ordered a basket of flowers to be delivered from you, so that will have been the first thing your mum saw when she woke up.'

Natalie glanced at Adam, amazed that a man with so much on his mind should have found the time to attend to such details.

Jane was indeed very tired when Natalie arrived on the ward.

'How are you?' Natalie smiled down at her.

'Sore.' Jane pulled a face. 'Is Timmy all right?'

'He's fine. We had a great time at the waxworks. He wanted to come and tell you all about it now, but Adam said no, as you'd be feeling very tired.'

'I guess I have Mr Curtis to thank for those.' Jane nodded at the basket of carnations on the locker beside her bed.

'He told Timothy he'd arranged for them to be sent from him—he's so kind, for such a busy man,' said Natalie.

'I'm glad you're noticing at last,' remarked Jane sleepily.

'Whatever do you mean?' Natalie stared at her.

'Well, it's becoming rather obvious that he's very fond of you.'

Natalie looked away in embarrassment, suddenly unable to meet Jane's gaze. 'I think you're mistaken,' she mumbled.

'I don't,' said Jane, fighting to keep her eyes open. 'I've never seen him as happy as he's been since you came on the scene.'

'I wouldn't be too sure that necessarily has anything to do with me,' said Natalie drily, recalling the tone of the blonde woman's voice when she had called Adam back into the drawing-room. 'And, besides, earlier on you said he was angry.'

'I think that might have been something to do with that Roger Lomax,' said Jane with a sleepy smile.

Natalie frowned. 'What makes you think that?'

'Well, after I'd told him you'd gone to the social

club last night he asked me if Mr Lomax had phoned or had come to pick you up.'

'Oh, did he? And what did you say?'

'I said not as far as I knew. He seemed pleased then, but this morning he was angry.'

'That was after he'd found me dancing with Roger Lomax,' said Natalie.

'Oh, dear.' Jane peered up at her short-sightedly, and she looked so worried that Natalie was forced to laugh.

'But I think you'll find things will be changing where Mr Lomax is concerned,' she said firmly, but later, after she had left Jane to sleep and was driving home, she found herself wondering about what Jane had said.

She had implied the same as Lyn Irving—that Adam's interest in her was more than professional and more than just family concern. As she approached Sheridan House she was aware that her heart was thudding, but still at the back of her mind hovered the memories of Suzanne and all she had meant to him, and, of more immediate concern, the woman who seemed to be in his life at the moment, whoever she was.

When she went indoors she was surprised to find Adam and Timothy seated at the kitchen table, deeply engrossed in a game of draughts.

'I was all set to prepare dinner,' said Adam, 'but Jane had beaten me to it and had made a chicken casserole. It's in the oven now.' He nodded towards the Aga as he spoke.

'Did you see my mum?' asked Timothy, peering up anxiously at Natalie through his glasses.

'I did. She's fine, and she sends her love,' replied Natalie. 'And she's looking forward to seeing you tomorrow.'

'Did you tell her all about the murderers?' he asked excitedly.

'Er—no, I thought perhaps you might like to do that,' she said with a laugh as she took off her coat and scarf, and, tossing her head, she ran her fingers through her thick hair. Suddenly she was aware that Adam was watching her. She felt the colour tinge her cheeks and in sudden confusion she looked away.

They ate their dinner with Timothy, right there in the kitchen, cosy in the warmth from the Aga, and while Natalie cleared the dishes Adam played another game of draughts with the little boy, allowing him to win this time. Afterwards Natalie supervised Timothy's bath, read him a story and tucked him up in bed with a goodnight kiss as she was sure Jane would have done.

Much later, still seated at the scrubbed pine table as they lingered over a second cup of coffee, Natalie found herself studying Adam's hands. The strong fingers were curled loosely around his mug, and she recalled the many other times when those same fingers had held surgical instruments, and she had watched mesmerised as he had exercised his great skill in saving someone's life.

It was then, when she was pleasantly preoccupied,

that Adam caught her unawares. Looking up from his coffee, he stared at her for a moment across the table, and there was something in the expression in his dark eyes that made her shiver slightly, then quietly he asked, 'Did you know he was married?'

CHAPTER NINE

FOR a moment Natalie simply stared at Adam, then as it slowly dawned on her what he meant she realised that, far from Adam not having seen Roger as she had at first thought, he had in fact seen and understood everything.

She sighed and looked down at the remains of her coffee in the bottom of her mug. 'No, I didn't know,' she said at last.

'Did he deliberately mislead you, or did he just omit to tell you that choice bit of information?'

Natalie glanced up sharply, for she was uncertain whether the edge in Adam's tone was one of sarcasm or disgust, but as her eyes met his she recognised a hint of sympathy.

She shook her head. 'I'm not sure really.' She hesitated. 'I can't really remember. I don't think he actually said he wasn't married. . . I just assumed. . . I suppose I'm just incredibly naïve.' She gave a short laugh.

Adam remained silent for a moment, then he stood up and, looking down at her, he said, 'Shall we go into the lounge? We'd be more comfortable in there.'

She nodded and silently followed him into the large elegant room on the first floor that overlooked the quiet square tucked away from the bustle of London's traffic. The olive-green velvet curtains were still open, something Jane would have seen to if she'd been there, and the room was lit by the eerie light of the street-lamps below.

Adam lit a couple of table lamps, drew the heavy curtains, then poured them both a brandy, while Natalie sank down into a corner of the cream leather sofa and rested her head against the soft back.

He handed her her drink, then stood watching her for a moment before he said, 'Has today upset you very much?'

'In what way?' She glanced up at him. 'The fact that he's married, or that he deceived me?'

'Either, or both if you like.' Adam cradled his glass in his hands and they both watched as the amber liquid swirled around. 'Let's take one at a time. How about the fact that he deceived you?'

'I'm angry that he deceived me,' said Natalie firmly.

'Good, that's a nice positive reaction. Now, how about the fact that he's married?'

'I despise that sort of behaviour,' she said flatly. In the silence that followed the only sound to be heard was the far-off wailing of a police siren.

'He'd made it perfectly plain he wanted a serious relationship,' she added after a few moments, then, studying the liquid in the bottom of her glass, she glanced up quickly at Adam. 'It looks as if your judgement of him was perfectly correct.'

Adam gave a slight shrug. He was standing in

front of the fireplace, and as he looked down at her, a thoughtful expression on his face, he rocked slightly on his heels.

'Well, I was right about the fact that he was after you and that he wanted more than the odd date, but I'm not really concerned with Lomax now one way or the other. What do concern me are your feelings. How do you feel about him? Apart from the fact that he amused you?' He allowed the flicker of a smile to touch his lips, then he immediately grew serious again as he waited for her reply. There was a sudden tension in the room, and it was almost as if he dreaded what he was about to hear.

At last Natalie drew a deep breath. 'Actually, Adam, that's about it, really—that and the fact that he was willing to talk about Pitlochry at a time when I was feeling particularly homesick.'

He stared at her as if he couldn't believe what she was saying, then carefully he set his glass down on the mantelpiece. 'Let me get this straight,' he said slowly. 'Are you saying that you were never interested in Roger Lomax?'

'Not in the way you mean, no.' She shook her head.

'So why in heaven's name didn't you say so? Why did you let me go on and make a complete and utter fool of myself?'

She shrugged and moved restlessly on the sofa. 'I was irritated by the way you were implying that I wasn't able to take care of myself, that there was something wrong with my judgement when it came to men.'

'And, as it turned out, I was right!' There was a note of exasperation in his tone now, then as he stared down at her his expression suddenly softened and, moving forward, he sat down beside her. 'I wish you'd told me you were feeling homesick,' he said softly. 'I could have talked to you about Scotland— far more than Lomax, as it turned out.'

In the long silence that followed Natalie fumbled to put her glass on a table by the side of the sofa, for quite suddenly she realised her hands were shaking. Then she felt Adam's arm go round her shoulders and when she turned her head she found his face very close to her own.

'I didn't think you'd want to be reminded of Scotland,' she whispered.

'Oh, Natalie,' he sighed, and briefly she saw the pain cross his features, then he lifted his hand and gently ran the backs of his fingers down the side of her face. 'You're quite beautiful, you know,' he went on as she listened in amazement. 'I couldn't believe it when I saw you at your brother's wedding. The last time I'd seen you you seemed little more than a child, but there I was, confronted by this vision of loveliness. . .' He moved his hand to touch her hair, allowing his fingers to become entangled in the silky red tendrils while the arm that was around her shoulders tightened as he drew her closer.

Helplessly she stared into his face, the strong

features, the dark eyes and brows and the hint of masculine shadow forming on his jaw. How often in the past when she'd been merely a girl she had gazed at him and adored him from afar, and now here she was, not only in his home but almost in his arms and with his mouth only inches from her own.

Her gaze came to rest wonderingly on his mouth, and she recalled his kiss and the feelings it had awakened, and suddenly she wanted him to do just that again; she wanted to feel the pressure of those firm, finely shaped lips on hers and to experience once again the fierce desire that had transmitted itself from his body to hers.

As he moved his hand from her hair and gently traced the outline of her lips with his fingers she leaned forward and, leaving him in no doubt of what she wanted, she parted her lips beneath his.

This time the desperate quality was missing from his kiss, but it was replaced by a tenderness that only lightly veiled the passion beneath. In a completely spontaneous movement Natalie wound her arms around his neck, burying her fingers in his thick dark hair as she hungrily responded. He smelt of some subtle expensive cologne which assailed her senses, and this, together with the light touch of his hands which now roamed tantalisingly over her body, evoked a heady sensation that filled her with longing.

For an indefinable period of time Natalie forgot everything as Adam reawakened half-remembered desires, then went on to stir some unleashed passion deep inside whose existence she'd never dreamt of.

Only once, when she realised he'd undone all the buttons on her blouse, did she falter and wonder what she was doing, but then when his hands cupped her breasts, the firm fingers caressing her to unimaginable heights of longing, she forgot her fears again and gave herself up to his demands.

As those demands became more urgent and she realised Adam's self-control was slipping they hurtled headlong towards that treacherous moment of no return, the moment when the mind lost its grip and the desires of the body had to be satisfied.

And it was just seconds away from that moment when Natalie heard a sound, and, turning her head sharply, she looked over the back of the sofa and saw Timothy standing in the open doorway. There were tears on his cheeks and he was rubbing his eyes. With almost superhuman strength she succeeded in pushing Adam away.

'What the hell. . .?' demanded Adam.

'It's Timothy,' she muttered as she desperately tried to rearrange her clothing.

Adam groaned and flung himself back on to the sofa, obviously fighting for control.

'What is it, Timmy? What's wrong?' By this time Natalie had scrambled to her feet.

'There's a nasty man in my room. . .' His breath caught in a sob.

'Oh, Timmy. . .' In a flash Natalie was beside him and, crouching down, she put her arms around him. 'You've had a bad dream—there's no man in your room, really there isn't. Come on, we'll go back together.' Taking his hand and not daring to look in Adam's direction, she left the room.

She made Timothy a glass of warm milk, then carefully searched his room so that he could accept that there really wasn't anyone there, then she tucked him up in bed again and sat with him until he fell asleep.

As she watched his eyelids grow heavy she wondered what would happen when she got back to the lounge, and with each passing moment she found she was delaying her return. She couldn't explain what had happened between herself and Adam, nor why it had happened, but it had very quickly escalated out of control.

Probably Adam was already regretting what had happened and was wondering how he could get out of the situation, as he was quite obviously heavily involved elsewhere.

Well, she thought as she finally stood up and looked down at the sleeping child, he needn't worry, she would make things easy for him. She knew he was only being kind to her and that she mustn't read any more into what had happened.

That she had found him even more attractive than she had ever imagined in her wildest of fantasies she knew she mustn't allow to affect her judgement. Hadn't she already made a fool of herself with Roger Lomax? If she wasn't very careful she would find herself in a similar situation, but this time with Adam Curtis.

She had been a fool to think she might have found

happiness with Adam, for what she hadn't accounted for had been the element of time. He was a vastly different man now from the young doctor she had known all those years ago and had adored from afar.

Squaring her shoulders, she flicked off Timothy's light switch and made her way slowly back to the lounge.

Adam was standing with his back to the door facing the fireplace, but he turned as she came into the room.

'Is he all right?' he asked.

'I think so,' she replied. 'I made him a drink and he's gone back to sleep now.'

'He certainly knows how to pick his moment,' Adam observed drily.

'Well, you were the one who said children loved to be frightened.' Natalie gave a wry smile, then paused. She hadn't come right back into the room and was still standing by the open door.

Taking a deep breath, she said, 'Adam, I think I'll get to bed now—it's been quite a day and I'm very tired.'

He stared at her and she was totally unable to interpret the expression in his eyes. For a moment she thought he was going to say something, to try to stop her in some way, then with a helpless shrug he turned away. 'Very well,' he said briefly.

Sleep, however, proved impossible, and Natalie tossed and turned for hours as she tried to come to terms with all that had happened. Then just before dawn she fell into an exhausted sleep and slept longer than she had intended, and when she finally dressed and went downstairs it was to find that Adam and Timothy had had breakfast and Adam was preparing to take the little boy to school.

'Would you be able to collect Jane?' he asked Natalie, and she thought she detected a coolness in his tone this morning.

'Of course,' she replied quickly. 'I'm hoping for a day off today. Will you be going in?' she added as an afterthought.

Adam nodded. 'Yes, I thought I would. Things are still far from normal and there's bound to be a full list. But I'd be grateful if you could help out here.'

He'd gone then, and she didn't see him again for the rest of that day. She did some shopping, tidied the house, then drove to the hospital to collect Jane.

Jane was still tired after her anaesthetic, and she made no protest when Natalie made her comfortable on the couch in her lounge. 'If you get plenty of rest at this stage you'll soon feel much better,' said Natalie. 'I'll make you some tea before I pick Timothy up from school, then when I get back I'll see about preparing dinner.'

Timothy was excited at the thought of seeing his mother, and he chattered non-stop on the way home from school. Natalie was quite happy to let him prattle on, but she found her thoughts wandering as she realised she would be cooking dinner for Adam that night. The thought made her apprehensive, but when they reached Sheridan House and Timothy had greeted his mother and told her all his news Jane said that Adam had phoned to say he would be dining out.

For the rest of the evening Natalie felt depressed as she was tormented by images of Adam with his glamorous girlfriend, then as she took in a cup of hot chocolate to Jane she suddenly couldn't bear it any longer.

'Did Adam say where he was dining?' she asked Jane as she straightened her pillows.

Jane shook her head. 'No, he didn't.' She glanced up anxiously at Natalie, and must have picked up something of her mood, for she said, 'But don't let it worry you—he gets invited to lots of dinner parties.'

'I can imagine.' Natalie perched on the edge of the bed. 'Like at the home of the blonde he brought here the other night?'

Jane frowned. 'A blonde, you say? I didn't see her.'

'No, you were in bed, but she was tall, sickeningly slim, and with masses of blonde hair.'

Jane was silent for a moment as if uncertain whether to say any more, and Natalie threw her a glance of pure misery.

'You mustn't take too much notice, you know,' Jane said at last. 'You'll find she's not important. She's one of many,' she said as Natalie's eyes opened wide in amazement.

'Whatever do you mean?'

'Exactly that. They come and go, but none of them ever lasts. His married friends are constantly trying to pair him off with one woman or another, but he never seems to allow himself to get close to any of them.'

At first Natalie was shocked by Jane's words, then the more she thought about it she became elated that there was no one serious in his life. But when the sudden euphoria had worn off she became convinced that James's opinion had probably been right and that Adam didn't allow himself to become involved because he wouldn't let anyone take Suzanne's place in his life.

This thought depressed her even more, then as she prepared for bed she contemplated the following day and her inevitable confrontation with Roger Lomax, and she felt her anger rising.

The first person she saw when she reached the theatre unit the following morning was her friend Lyn Irving who took one look at her and demanded to know what was wrong.

'What do you mean?' Natalie played for time as she sorted through the operating schedules on her desk.

'Well, there's obviously something up. You just don't look yourself—you're not going down with this flu, are you?' Lyn looked searchingly at her, then when Natalie shook her head she said quietly, 'Natalie, is it anything to do with Roger Lomax?'

Natalie shrugged. 'What makes you think that?'

She wasn't in fact entirely sure if her present frame of mind was to do with Roger Lomax or with Adam Curtis, but she could hardly say that to Lyn, who would think she was some sort of man-eater.

Lyn turned and closed the office door in an attempt to shut out any unwelcome intrusions, then she perched on the edge of Natalie's desk. 'Nat,' she began uncertainly, 'I think there's something you should know about Roger Lomax before you get too involved.'

'Like the fact that he's married?' asked Natalie quietly.

Lyn stared at her in amazement. 'You mean you know. . .?' When Natalie nodded she gave a low whistle. 'I'm sorry, Nat, I really didn't think you could know. I didn't think you were the type to let yourself get involved with a married man. . .'

'I didn't know. I only found out a couple of days ago.'

Lyn's eyes opened even wider. 'How?'

'I saw him with his wife. . .and his children.'

'But I understood his family were in Liverpool.'

'I can assure you, the day before yesterday they were in London—seeing the sights.' Natalie shrugged and began putting the papers on her desk into folders.

They remained silent for a few moments, then Lyn said, 'Do you feel very badly about it?'

'I feel angry about the way he tried to chat me up. But that's all. He simply wasn't my type, although I was prepared to be friends with him.

There's no chance of that now,' Natalie said grimly, 'and I shall tell him so when I see him.'

'That may be sooner than you think,' said Lyn, pulling a face.

'What do you mean?'

'He's taken up Adam Curtis's invitation to spend the morning in Theatre to see how staff shortages affect the routine.' As she spoke Lyn threw Natalie an apprehensive glance.

'That's all I need this morning!' Natalie sighed, and slapped the pile of folders down on to the desk. 'What's the list, Lyn? Let's hope it's something really gory for Mr Lomax to watch.'

Lyn grinned. 'Will a prostatectomy and a AP resection do for starters?'

'I should think so,' replied Natalie crisply. 'How are we off for staff?'

'One ODA short at the moment in theatre two; otherwise we're up to strength.'

'Huh, that's a pity. He should have been here when we were three short,' observed Natalie. 'Has Mr Curtis arrived yet?' she added.

'Yes, I think he's scrubbing up,' replied Lyn.

'Right, let's get this show on the road, then, shall we?'

'Natalie do you want me to look after Roger Lomax?' There was an anxious expression on Lyn's face as she spoke.

'I wouldn't dream of it,' replied Natalie. 'As I'm theatre sister, visitors are my responsibility. In fact, I could quite enjoy this.' With her head high she marched out of the office and almost collided with a figure who was standing outside, his hand raised ready to knock on the door.

'Ah, Mr Lomax, talk of the devil,' said Natalie coolly as she briefly allowed her eyes to met his. 'We were just discussing you. Staff Nurse Irving has told me of your proposed visit this morning, and we've decided to take you along to visit each of the theatres to conduct your time and motion study.'

'Thank you, Sister,' he replied, then added, 'but it's hardly a time and motion study.'

'Really?' Natalie raised her eyebrows and in the same cool tone as before said, 'I was under the impression that that was exactly what it was. We say we need more staff. You say we don't. You've come along to try to prove your point—what could be more of a time and motion study than that? Now, we have a very tight schedule ahead of us,' she concluded crisply, 'so, if you'd like to come along, we'll get you gowned up for Theatre.'

As she marched ahead of him down the corridor Natalie was aware that Roger was almost running to keep up with her, and as they reached the scrub-rooms he grabbed the door-handle and held the door shut so that she was forced to wait. 'Natalie, please,' he almost gasped.

She stood motionless, her head averted, as she waited for him to open the door.

'Listen, Natalie. We have to talk. . .'

'What about?' Her tone was icy, and when he stared at her speechlessly she said, 'I can't imagine we've anything to say to each other. Now, if you don't mind, would you please open the door? I have work to do.'

'But you must let me explain. . .' He trailed off as Jon Bell suddenly appeared and he was forced to stand aside while the anaesthetist opened the door and stood back for Natalie to precede him into the scrub-room.

Much to Natalie's relief there was no further opportunity for conversation with Roger, as the consultants were already present and preparing for their morning lists. First she took him on a conducted tour of the three theatres that came under her supervision, explaining the roles of each of the team members as she went, then they went back to theatre one, where Peter Farmer was performng a transurethral prostatectomy.

'This elderly patient has an enlarged prostate gland, which is obstructing the flow of urine,' she explained as they stood at the back of the theatre and watched the team in action. 'As you can see, he hasn't had a general anaesthetic but an epidural.'

'You mean he's awake?' muttered Roger from behind his mask.

'That's right.' Natalie nodded. 'The operation is carried out endoscopically—it's far better for the patient, as he can be mobilised more quickly afterwards.'

They watched as the various members of the team went about their duties, then Roger said, 'Do you have your full staff quota here this morning?'

'Yes,' replied Natalie. 'In this theatre we do, but, as you can see, everyone has their duties, and if we're only one short it can make a vast difference. In a moment I'll take you to theatre two, where Mr Curtis is operating. There's an ODA off sick there this morning with no one to replace her, so you'll be able to judge for yourself.'

As they arrived at theatre two Adam was waiting to begin operating on a middle-aged lady requiring a colostomy. The ODAs were wheeling the anaesthetised patient into the theatre and the theatre staff were preparing the instruments and equipment; the heart monitor, the diathermy machine and the sterile green towels used to cover the patient.

Adam was studying the patient's X-rays in a lighted viewing box, but he looked up as Natalie ushered Roger inside the double doors.

'Ah, Mr Lomax, you've come to join us, I see,' said Adam. 'Have you watched major surgery before?'

Roger shook his head.

'No? That's a pity. I always think you managers should be aware of what goes on on the other side of the fence,' said Adam smoothly. 'Now, are we ready? Dr Bell? Sister Fraser? Good, we'll begin.' For a fraction of a second his eyes met Natalie's above their masks, then, turning to his scrub nurse, he said, 'Scalpel, please, Nurse.'

CHAPTER TEN

As THE operation for the resection of the patient's colon progressed Natalie became involved in her normal theatre routine plus the organisation of the work of the missing ODA, and in a short while she had forgotten that Roger Lomax was even present.

There were complications with excessive bleeding and breathing problems for the patient, and Natalie had no time to worry about onlookers, then, when it was almost over and she was watching Adam as he sutured the wound, it was he who remembered.

He glanced up as he returned a pair of forceps to the scrub nurse, first to check the swab rack where the swabs that had been used during the operation were accounted for, then to the far side of the theatre.

'It looks as if Mr Lomax has had enough, Sister,' he remarked impassively.

Natalie turned sharply and saw that Roger had indeed left the theatre.

'I didn't know he'd gone,' she said. Then, looking around at the rest of the team, she asked, 'Did anyone see him go?'

'He was looking a bit green at the time of the incision,' said Jon Bell with a chuckle. 'But I think it was the haemorrhage that finally did it.'

'Just as long as he saw enough to convince him that we need more staff,' said Adam as he finished suturing and stepped back from the table.

'I'd better go and see where he is,' said Natalie and, slipping from the theatre, she peeled off her gloves and discarded her mask and cap. She found Roger in her office. He was sitting by an open window, and she noticed he looked very pale.

'Are you all right?' she asked briskly.

He swallowed, then nodded without speaking.

'Have you been in here long? I didn't notice you leaving the theatre.'

'Oh, about half an hour or so.' He tried to sound casual. 'It might have been longer, but I had to leave; it got so hot in there.'

She nodded. 'I couldn't come out any sooner—we were far too busy, as you no doubt noticed,' she added pointedly.

'Yes, Natalie, I noticed, and you've proved your point. I'll have your staff quota reviewed at the next management meeting.'

'Thank you, Roger, she replied briefly. There was an awkward little silence, then she said, 'Well, if you'll excuse me, I have some paperwork to do.'

He didn't move from his chair, however, and, staring up at her, he said, 'Just a moment, Natalie. I must talk to you.'

She stiffened. 'I told you, Roger, I don't think we've got any more to say to each other.'

'But we have. I want to explain to you about the other day.'

'As far as I can see, there's nothing to explain.'

'But you don't understand. . .' He broke off as a student nurse put her head round the door and asked Natalie if she had a certain patient's set of notes.

'Just a moment, Jenny.' Natalie crossed to the filing cabinet, where she found the required file and handed it to the girl. All the while she was uncomfortably aware of Roger's gaze upon her.

When the student had gone, shutting the door behind her, Roger continued. 'I want to explain about what you saw in the waxworks.'

'You don't have to explain, Roger. I know exactly what I saw,' said Natalie coldly.

'But it isn't what you think. . .'

'What isn't? The fact that you have a wife and—two daughters, is it? Or are there more?'

'No, what I meant was, you don't understand about my wife and me. Things haven't been right. . .'

'Oh, surely you're not going to give me that old "my wife doesn't understand me" routine,' she said witheringly. 'I'd have thought you could come up with something better than that, Roger. After all, I'd imagine you've had plenty of practice.'

He stared at her. 'Hey, what do you mean? What do you take me for?'

'I really don't know. Apart from the fact, of course, that you're a cheat and a liar—other than that, I'm not sure. You'll have to enlighten me. In fact, I probably wouldn't have found out as much as that if it hadn't been for that amazing coincidence in the Chamber of Horrors. Quite an appropriate venue, as it turned out, I thought.'

'If it hadn't been for you mentioning waxworks in relation to that wretched child and putting the idea in my head I'd never have taken them there,' he muttered angrily. 'I never dreamt you intended going there as well.'

'And what would have happened if I hadn't been there? If I hadn't seen you?' she demanded angrily.

He stared at her, then shruggled helplessly, and she found herself thinking how glad she was that she hadn't become involved with him. He was acting now like a naughty schoolboy who had been caught out in some misdemeanour.

'I suppose we'd have carried on as we were,' he said, and as she caught her breath he added, 'What you don't seem to realise, Natalie, is just how much I think of you.'

'But you're married, for God's sake!'

'I wouldn't exactly be the first married man that this has happened to—it happens quite frequently, or have you still been living in the Dark Ages up there, north of the Border?'

Natalie could feel her anger rising, and, holding on to her temper with difficulty, she said, 'No, I haven't been living in the Dark Ages, as you put it, but I do have a few values left, even if they seem outdated to you, and one of them is that I make it a rule never to get involved with married men.'

'Couldn't you make an exception this time?' His

voice had taken on a pleading note, and as she gazed at him in exasperation he carried on, 'I told you, Natalie, I've wanted you from the moment I saw you. I can't help the way I feel any more than I can help the fact that I'm married.'

'And what about your wife? Wherever would she fit into your schemes?' A note of incredulity had entered her voice, but Roger didn't seem to notice and he looked up quickly as if her question indicated that she was trying to find a solution.

'I wouldn't want to hurt Margaret. . .'

'Oh, of course not. . .'

'She'll soon be moving down here from Liverpool, but if we're careful she needn't find out. London's a big place, and eventually we could work something out.'

'Will you please stop talking about "us"? There was never any such situation and there never will be.' Natalie was having difficulty holding on to her temper now, her face was flushed and her eyes glittering, but Roger must have misunderstood her emotions, for he stood up and began walking round the desk towards her. 'Please, Natalie. . .' he said.

He was breathing heavily, and as he approached she took a few steps backwards. 'Roger, you've got to understand there's absolutely no chance. . .' she began, suddenly alarmed by the look on his face.

'Why? Tell me why.' His voice was thick and urgent, and she shuddered. He was very close to her and she could feel his breath on her cheek. 'You know you wanted it as much as I did,' he muttered, and when she turned her head away from him in desperation he demanded, 'Aren't I good enough for you? Too rough, am I? Funny thing, I always imagined that's what you'd like—a bit of rough.' Reaching out his hand, he caught her chin and tried to twist her face towards him.

'Leave me alone,' she gasped.

'Playing the innocent now, are we?' His tone was ugly. 'Your type usually can't get enough—or is it that you're already getting it? Is it your fancy surgeon who's giving it to you? "I'm not living with him",' he mimicked her voice. 'Believe that and you'll believe anything! He's had the hots for you since you arrived, and don't bother trying to deny it.'

By this time he'd pinned Natalie in the corner of the office, and at the very moment that he would have finally grabbed her the door opened behind him, and to her overwhelming relief she saw Adam standing in the doorway.

He seemed to sum up the situation immediately. 'Get out, Lomax,' he said, and his voice cut the air like a rapier, 'and don't bother Sister Fraser again. If you do, you'll have me to answer to.'

For one moment Natalie thought there was going to be a show-down between the two men as, still dressed in theatre greens, they stood facing each other across the office. Roger Lomax was still breathing heavily and there were beads of perspiration on his upper lip, then finally an ugly expression crossed his features and, as if he knew he was beaten, he pushed past Adam through the doorway and disappeared down the corridor.

Natalie gave a great sigh of relief and held on to the edge of the desk for support. 'Thank you, Adam,' she whispered.

'Are you all right?' Lightly he touched her shoulder and quite suddenly all she wanted was for him to take her in his arms so she could rest her head on his chest.

'I don't think he'll bother you again,' he said grimly. 'But if he does, let me know. What was his game, anyway?'

'He seemed to think the fact that he has a wife and children shouldn't interfere with any relationship we might have been going to have.'

'I imagined it was something like that,' said Adam with a nod. 'That's why I came in.'

At that moment the telephone on her desk rang and Natalie leaned forward to answer it. As she did so she realised her hands were trembling, and she had to make a conscious effort to pull herself together.

It was an outside line, and as the girl on the switchboard was connecting her with the caller Natalie put her hand over the mouthpiece and said shakily, 'One thing is that I think the spell in Theatre might have done some good—he more or less promised more staff—mind you,' she grimaced, 'he might have changed his mind now. . .' Then, hearing that she was through to the caller, she took her hand from the mouthpiece. 'Hello?' she said, wondering who could be calling from outside the hospital. 'Natalie Fraser speaking.'

'Hello, Natalie,' a familiar male voice answered. 'It's James.'

'James,' she cried. 'What a lovely surprise! How are you?' She glanced up at Adam, who had been about to leave the room but had paused in the doorway when she had mentioned her brother's name.

'Natalie, I'm fine, but I'm afraid I have some bad news. . .'

'Is it Dad?' she said, her heart lurching.

'Yes, Nat, I'm afraid it is. He had a coronary this morning. He's in Intensive Care. I'm ringing from the hospital. I can't tell you much more at the moment except that his condition is critical.'

She was silent as a multitude of emotions teemed through her mind and she tried to grasp what had happened.

'Natalie, are you still there? Nat. . .?' James sounded anxious.

'Yes, yes, I'm here,' she said faintly.

'I wasn't sure what you'd want to do.'

'I want to come home.'

'Yes, of course, I thought you'd say that. But will you be able to? It's so soon after starting your job. . .'

'I'll have to try and work something out.' Her voice shook. 'I must be there, James—I must.'

As the tears filled her eyes she was aware of the receiver being taken from her grasp, then Adam was saying, 'Hello, James, it's Adam. What's happened?'

He listened in silence while James explained, then Natalie heard him say, 'There's no problem. She can come immediately. I'll book a flight now. Can we ring you back in about an hour?'

She looked up through her tears as he replaced the receiver.

'Get changed,' he said decisively. 'Give me half an hour, then I'll take you back to Sheridan House to pack a bag.'

She was more than happy to let him make the necessary arrangements, and it wasn't until they were almost back at Sheridan House that she questioned how he had secured time off for her.

'Don't worry about it,' he replied briefly. 'You've done more than your fair share recently.'

'I have to go, Adam,' she said, repeating what she had said to James. 'I have to be there. . .if anything happens to him. . .' She bit her lip and looked out of the window.

The weather had brightened in the last couple of days from the damp chill of February to blustery periods with sudden bursts of sunshine. The bulbs in the London parks were bursting into bloom in promise of the spring to come, but Natalie saw nothing that day, for her thoughts were far away at her home in Scotland.

When they reached Sheridan House Adam explained to Jane what had happened while Natalie went to her room to pack a bag and change into a comfortable tweed suit and high leather boots. When she was ready she fastened a Paisley scarf at her neck, then, draping a light-coloured trench coat round her shoulders, she picked up her bag and stepped out of her room on to the landing.

She immediately heard Adam talking on the telephone, but because he was speaking from his study and not from the phone in the hall the sound was slightly muffled and she couldn't distinguish what was being said. By the time she reached the foot of the stairs, however, he was waiting for her in the hall. Vaguely she noticed he had changed from his suit into cords and a Barbour jacket.

'I've booked a flight at four o'clock to Edinburgh,' he said. 'I've just spoken to James and he'll be there to meet the flight.' He glanced at his watch. 'Are you ready?' he asked, and when she nodded he said, 'We'd better be going in case the traffic's heavy between here and the airport.'

Natalie felt as if she were in a dream and that any moment she would wake up. She turned to say goodbye to Jane.

'I hope things won't be too bad,' said Jane sympathetically.

'Thank you, Jane. Say goodbye to Timothy for me.' Natalie hesitated in the doorway while Adam stowed her bag in the boot of the car.

'I will. Take care and hurry back.'

When Natalie looked up she realised Adam was waiting for her with the passenger door open, and moments later she was beside him, Jane had waved farewell and they were gathering speed on their way to Heathrow.

When they arrived at the terminal for the scheduled domestic flight to Edinburgh Natalie's mind was still in such a turmoil that she was pleased to sit in the airport lounge while Adam parked the car and collected her ticket and boarding pass. She was totally oblivious to the hubbub of the busy airport around her, and all she could think about was what she would find when she arrived in Scotland.

She knew her father's health had been failing for some time, and it had been this that had finally persuaded him to hand over the Pitlochry practice to James. They had all hoped that the reduction of work and of the stress his job invariably brought would improve his health. Now, it seemed, the unthinkable had happened and he had suffered the attack they had all feared.

James had said his condition was critical, and Natalie knew that could mean anything. How often in the past she herself had given that sort of statement to an anxious relative, and, although she had always tried to show compassion, now that it was her turn to agonise she realised that no one really knew what another suffered until they had experienced a similar situation.

She became so lost in her thoughts that she didn't know Adam had returned until he suddenly sat down beside her.

'The flight announcement has just come up on the screen,' he said quietly. 'Shall we go?'

She stood up and went to pick up her bag, but found that Adam had beaten her to it. 'You won't be able to come any further,' she said.

'Yes, I will,' he replied calmly.

It was only then that she realised that he was carrying a leather holdall in his other hand. Her eyes widened and he smiled. 'You didn't think I'd let you go alone, did you?'

Suddenly she felt overwhelmed by a rush of emotion that she was totally at a loss to explain.

When they were seated on the plane just before take-off Natalie glanced at Adam. 'How did you manage to arrange your absence?' she asked.

'With the same reason as you—I figure I have some time owing me.' Then when he saw her expression he gave a wry smile. 'Seriously, things are all right. Both Uri and Peter Farmer are available, and they can call in Souter in an emergency.'

'But what about the flu epidemic?'

'Fortunately it seems to be on the wane. I'm sure the worst is over.' He leaned across her to see out of the window. 'Here we go,' he said as the plane finished taxiing and gathered speed for take-off.

As they left the ground he said, 'Didn't you want me to come with you?'

'Of course I did. I was never more relieved in my life than when you said you were coming. You'll never know how grateful I am to you for arranging everything, Adam.' Natalie swallowed and blinked. 'I seemed to go into a state of shock after James phoned. I think I'd have been incapable of organising anything. If it had been left to me I'd probably have attempted to drive up.'

'That was what I wanted to avoid,' he said. 'You wouldn't have been in any fit state to drive, especially where you're worrying so much. I thought about driving you myself, but this way seemed more sensible, and of course it's much faster.'

'I hope it'll be fast enough. I just hope I'll be in time.'

'I'm sure you will,' he replied reassuringly. 'Your father's a tough one, you know—I'm sure he'll pull through.'

'Did James say any more when you phoned back?' she asked a little later.

'Not very much, except that the house in Pitlochry is in uproar.'

'Oh, why is that?'

'They have the decorators in, apparently. It hardly seemed fair to descend on them, so I've taken the liberty of booking us both into Craigie Court. I hope you approve.'

She threw him another glance. 'You seem to have thought of everything,' she said quietly.

'It isn't the first time I've had to deal with an emergency situation,' he said.

'No, of course not, I was forgetting. It must have been terrible for you at the time of Suzanne's accident.' She looked curiously at him. 'Did you have anyone to help you, or did you have to see to everything yourself?'

He didn't answer immediately, and Natalie was

just beginning to wish she'd kept quiet when he said, 'Actually, I wasn't referring to Suzanne's accident when I talked of emergency situations. I was merely referring to my work.'

'Oh, I'm sorry—I thought. . .'

He carried on as if she hadn't spoken, 'Although you were quite right, of course, that was an emergency, and yes, I did have to cope in somewhat unusual circumstances. Friends helped, naturally, but. . .' He shrugged.

'I am sorry, Adam, I should never have mentioned it. I know how much you loved her and how much it must hurt to talk about her.'

They were mostly silent after that for the rest of the short flight, but there had been something in Adam's manner when he had spoken of Suzanne's accident that had intrigued Natalie. She knew she wasn't in any frame of mind at the present to try to analyse what it had been, but she put it to the back of her mind with the promise that she would think about it again when her present crisis was over.

When they landed at Edinburgh Airport James was there to meet them in his Land Rover. Natalie almost fell into his arms.

'Is there any more news?' she asked, looking up anxiously into her brother's face and dreading what she might see there.

But he shook his head. 'No, nothing new,' he said quietly, then, turning to Adam, he added, 'Thanks for coming, old man; it's really good of you.'

'Not at all. It was the least I could do,' Adam replied as he stowed their bags in the back of the Land Rover and they took their places, ready for the drive north.

CHAPTER ELEVEN

THE promise of spring came later in Scotland than in the slightly warmer south, but, although there were as yet no signs of colour in the wild, dramatic landscape, it held a beauty all its own.

As they travelled north to Pitlochry Natalie, in spite of her anguish over her father, felt an odd sort of calm descend on her, the sense of calm that always came with being in her beloved birthplace, and as they sped through the deepening Scottish twilight she found herself peering into the gloom, looking for familiar landmarks.

Once she turned and found Adam watching her intently, and as their eyes met she knew he too was thinking of the moment they had been so close, when, if Timothy hadn't interrupted, they would doubtless have made love.

So much had happened since then that it had left her thoughts tangled and confused. First had come Jane's revelation that the blonde woman was one of many. That in itself had been a shock, but then, when she had explained that Adam never allowed any relationship to get serious, it made sense, because it fitted the theory that he couldn't find anyone to take Suzanne's place.

And if that was the case, what chance did she

stand when the likes of the glamorous woman she'd
seen at Sheridan House didn't qualify? As if all that
hadn't been enough, hot on its heels had come the
show-down with Roger Lomax, but, traumatic as
that had been, it had left Natalie feeling relieved
that the whole thing was over.

She hadn't really been attracted to Roger in the
first place, and somehow, without her realising it,
the whole thing had blown up out of all proportion.
She wondered what Adam thought now that he
knew Roger hadn't meant anything to her, and she
stole another glance at him, but this time his profile
was turned away from her and he was staring out of
the window. It had been cold and blustery at the
airport and the wind had caught his hair, ruffling it
so that it gave him a boyish look.

With a pang Natalie wondered what he was
thinking. Was he remembering other times he had
travelled this road with James? In particular the
time he had come to Pitlochry for Christmas, the
time she had been overjoyed, only to have her
hopes dashed the moment he'd set eyes on Suzanne.
After that things had never been quite the same
again.

They were all three very quiet on the drive, then,
as they were travelling on the final stretch of road
approaching Pitlochry, James said, 'We'll go straight
to the hospital. I'll see what the situation is, but if
you want to stay, Natalie, I'll have to leave you
there. I must get back for evening surgery—I've
already had to cancel one surgery today. Kirsty's at

home, taking calls, but she's having to divert any urgent ones directly to Casualty.'

'Of course,' Natalie replied, then glanced up sharply as they swung into the familiar gates of the hospital where until so recently she had been a theatre sister.

With a growing feeling of dread she climbed out of the Land Rover, and with Adam close behind her she followed James into the coronary care unit.

Natalie knew the sister on CCU very well, for not only had she worked with Roz Stobart, but they had also done their training in the same hospital in Edinburgh. After James had introduced Adam the three of them were shown through to the small side-ward where Iain Fraser was being cared for.

'His condition is still very critical,' explained Roz. 'I'm afraid his heartbeat is unstable and fibrillating. Perhaps you'd like to stay with him while I tell Mr Rickard, the consultant, that you've arrived.'

Natalie felt her stomach churn as she approached the bed where her father lay. He was wired to a heart monitor, and a saline drip was being administered intravenously. He was totally unaware of their arrival, and Natalie looked anxiously at James.

He picked up the drug chart from the foot of the bed and studied it. 'He's on diamorphine and heparin as an anticoagulant.'

Her father looked old and very vulnerable with his chest bare, exposing the patches attached to the heart monitor. Natalie felt a lump rise in her throat as she picked up his hand where it lay on the striped hospital bedspread and gently stroked it.

'Oh, Dad,' she whispered, and the tears that had threatened for so long finally overflowed and spilled down her cheeks. James slipped his arm round her shoulders and hugged her, and the two of them stood for a quiet moment looking down at their father.

Adam stood back, respecting their need for a moment's privacy, then Roz Stobart appeared again and informed them that Mr Rickard was in her office.

'I want to see him,' said James. 'Perhaps you'd like to come with me, Adam?'

Adam nodded. 'Of course. I've heard of Rickard; he's an excellent man. Do you want to come, Natalie?'

She shook her head. 'No, I'll stay here. You two go—I know you'll ask all the right questions.'

'I'll organise some tea,' said Roz and the three of them left the ward, leaving Natalie alone with her father. With a sigh she took off her coat, then, drawing up a chair to the side of the bed, she sat down and again took her father's hand in hers.

For a long time she simply sat and watched him. His hair was ruffled and she noticed how white it had become over the past few months, unlike the hair on his chest, which was still iron-grey. He had grown old almost without her being aware of it, and suddenly, unreasonably she felt a surge of anger because he might be about to die and leave her.

Then her anger turned to tears that dropped silently on to the hand that clasped his and trickled through their fingers on to the bedspread.

Her vigil lasted for the best part of the night. Long after James had left to tend to his own patients she sat on, silently watching the figure on the bed. She watched as the nursing staff went about their duties, turning their patient every few hours to prevent bedsores, and as the duty doctor inserted a catheter to relieve fluid retention.

She watched as his medication was administered and throughout it all she was aware that Adam had stayed with her. Sometimes he sat in a chair in the corner of the room, at other times he disappeared for a while, but she felt his nearness acutely and was comforted by it.

Later she was to learn that his presence in the hospital had caused quite a stir and several of the staff had been keen to meet him, but primarily he was there only for her.

Then in the small hours of the morning the sister on night duty touched her lightly on the shoulder. 'Why don't you try and get a little rest, Miss Fraser?' she asked kindly.

'I'm all right. . .' began Natalie.

'You look exhausted. Come into my office and lie down for a bit on the couch. I promise I'll call you if there's any change.'

Then a little after dawn, as the sky slowly lightened, Adam gently awakened her. For a moment she couldn't think where she was, she only knew that it seemed the most natural thing in the world to find him there, close beside her, when she awoke.

Then she remembered, and she started up in alarm.

'What is it? What's happened?' she gasped.

'It's all right,' he said gently. 'I think he's turned the corner. He's much better; Rickard is very optimistic.'

'Oh, thank God,' she whispered, then, struggling to get up, she said. 'I must see him.'

Her father was awake, and this time when she took his hand he gently squeezed hers in response. It wasn't much and he was very weak, but it was enough to let Natalie know that he knew she was there.

Iain Fraser's condition continued to improve, and by midday, when James and Kirsty arrived, Natalie felt able to leave the hospital for a while. Adam hired a taxi, which took them both to Craigie Court.

There were mostly silent as the taxi approached the country hotel, but Natalie was beginning to feel quietly optimistic about her father's condition. She had spoken briefly to Mr Rickard before she'd left the hospital, and his attitude had been encouraging. He too had been eager to talk to Adam, and Natalie realised in just how much esteem Adam was held, and she felt a moment's pride in the fact that she worked with him. As the car crunched to a halt in the forecourt of the hotel she also found herself wondering anew at his apparent concern for her.

To her surprise, Adam had reserved a suite.

'You needn't have gone to all this trouble,' she said as she glanced round the luxurious sitting-room on the first floor of the beautiful old mansion while a porter carried up their bags.

'If we're going to be here for a few days I thought we might as well be comfortable,' he said calmly as he tipped the porter and closed the door behind him. 'And you needn't worry what people will think, because there are two bedrooms.' There was a hint of amusement in his voice as he crossed the room and flung open two doors on the far side. Natalie caught a glimpse of delicately furnished bedrooms with high arched windows draped in apricot net.

'Of course I'm not worried about that,' she said. 'I've learnt that people think what they want. Besides, I should imagine that the entire hospital knows by now that I'm living with you.'

Adam smiled. 'They may assume that, but you and I know, in the real sense of the word, it isn't true, don't we?' He stared down at her for a moment and she found herself holding her breath as she thought he was going to say more, but, changing the subject, he said briskly, 'Now, may I suggest that we go downstairs and have some lunch, because I'm absolutely starving?'

Natalie had thought she wouldn't be able to eat a thing, but when she saw the mouth-watering buffet laid out in the hotel dining-room she realised she too was ravenously hungry. They made their selection from a range of seafoods, cold roast meats, game and poultry, Scottish salmon and trout and an

intriguing variety of salads. Adam ordered a bottle
of wine to go with their meal, and it was later, as
they lingered over coffee, that he leaned back in his
chair and said, 'I shall need some fresh air after that
lot.'

'Me too.' She smiled, feeling more relaxed than
she had been for weeks. 'How about a walk down
to the loch?'

'Good idea.'

'After that I must go back to the hospital for a
while,' she added.

He nodded. 'I thought that was what you'd want.
Shall I reserve a table for dinner?'

'Actually, James and Kirsty have asked us to have
a meal with them.'

He hesitated fractionally and she threw him an
anxious glance, wondering if he would object, but
his expression remained inscrutable. 'Fine,' he said
briefly, then he stood up. 'I should think you'll need
a coat,' he added as he glanced out of the window.
In spite of the fact that it was a clear, bright March
day with fluffy clouds that scurried across a wide
blue sky, there was still a decided chill in the air.

They left the hotel dining-room and made their
way back to their suite to collect their coats. Natalie
was feeling happier than she had for some considerable time, and as they stepped out of the lift she
told Adam again how grateful she was to him for
coming with her to Scotland.

'It's been such a help to know that you've been

there taking care of everything,' she said as he inserted the key in the door of their suite.

The door swung open and he stood back for her to procede him, then he said lightly, 'Don't mention it. Glad to be of service, ma'am.'

As she passed him her shoulder brushed his chest, and she looked up at him and in a purely involuntary movement she reached up and kissed his cheek in a token of thanks.

Afterwards, if anyone had asked Natalie what happened next, the exact sequence of events, she would have been hard pushed to remember, for everything seemed to happen as if in a dream.

One minute she was in the open doorway on tiptoe, kissing Adam's cheek, then she was in his arms and he had kicked the door shut behind them and was kissing her, but this was no light peck on the cheek; this was a fierce, crushing kiss, as if he was unleashing a passion that had been restrained for a very long time.

'Oh, Natalie.' He groaned as he caught her face between his hands, burying his strong surgeon's fingers in her silky hair while his mouth sought every inch of her face, her forehead, her cheeks, her eyelids, and finally taking command once again of her mouth.

If she had attempted to protest it would have been lost in the onslaught, but as his actions became more demanding with each passing second Natalie knew that protest was the furthest thing from her mind.

The urgency of his desire increased, becoming more and more obvious as he pressed against her and her own passions rose to fever pitch as they had done once before. On that occasion their desires had remained unfulfilled, but this time Natalie soon realised that Adam was not going to let that happen again when he effortlessly lifted her up and carried her to the bed in his room.

He undressed her in an agony of suspense, removing each item of her clothing until she was quite naked, then, pausing only briefly to adore and wonderingly caress the smooth contours of her body, he quickly discarded his own clothes.

Then for Natalie came that exquisite moment, the moment she had dreamed of but despaired would ever happen, when he lowered himself on to her, their bodies met and their flesh merged.

So great was his desire, his need for her, that almost as soon as he began moving he had difficulty restraining himself, and it was over quickly—too quickly.

'I'm sorry,' he whispered as she held him against her. 'You're so incredibly beautiful. . . I'm sorry.'

'It's all right,' she reassured him, holding his head cradled against her breasts.

But moments later he began caressing her as if to make amends for his impatience, and for the next hour, with mouth and fingertips, he aroused her to heights of desire that she had never dreamed of, covering every inch of her body, so that in the end it was she who begged for sweet release.

And this time when he claimed her he held her there on the brink of ecstasy until they soared together.

Later, in the glorious aftermath of lovemaking, they lay in each other's arms, reflecting.

'Actually,' said Adam, 'that was the last thing I expected to happen.'

'You mean it was totally unpremeditated?' Natalie rolled away from him and, propping herself on one elbow, looked down at him.

'Absolutely,' he replied. But, while his expression was deadly serious, she detected a glimmer of amusement in his dark eyes.

'Liar!' She laughed and pushed back the thick curtain of her hair that had fallen across her face.

Stretching out his hand, Adam gently traced a line down her cheek, under her chin, across her shoulder, only stopping as he cupped her breast. 'I don't know what you mean. After all, I reserved two rooms.' Then, growing serious, he asked softly, 'Any regrets?' while she shivered in delight at his touch.

'Of course not. How could I possibly regret what we've just done?'

'But?' He raised his eyebrows as his fingers continued to tease and caress.

'But what?'

'From the tone of your voice, I would have said a "but" was about to follow.'

Natalie sighed. 'Would you?' Leaning forward, she in turn began to trace patterns, this time around his mouth, following the outline of his lips. 'I don't know, Adam, I just don't know. I certainly didn't plan this, but it's happened, and it was wonderful.' She gave a little gasp as his hand left her breast and began travelling downwards, and as she felt the involuntary response from his own body she knew he was ready for her again, and for the moment she decided that any fears or worries would just have to wait.

CHAPTER TWELVE

MUCH later Adam suggested that they take their walk to the loch. 'We need to talk,' he admitted, 'I know that, but I can't see how we're ever going to have a sensible conversation here in this room.'

Natalie laughed and went to dress, and a little later they left the hotel terrace hand in hand, crossed the lawns and took the path beneath the trees to the loch. They walked in silence for a while, and she was reminded of the last time they had taken this path. So much had happened since then that it was almost impossible to recall just how she had felt on that occasion.

As if he could read her thoughts Adam suddenly said, 'I can't believe it was only a few months ago that we walked down here.' He nodded towards the strip of water shining in the sunlight that had just become visible between the dark green pines.

'Nor me,' she agreed. 'If anyone had told me then all that was going to happen I would never have believed them. I was convinced then that my life was mapped out for me, that I was secure in my job and that I'd never leave Scotland.'

'And have you regretted it? Leaving Scotland, I mean?' he asked.

'I don't think so. I've missed it, and I've been

homesick, as I told you, but I can't say I've regretted it. I enjoy the job, Adam, it's been a challenge, and I've met some lovely people—Jane, Timothy, Lyn Irving. . .'

'Pity about Lomax,' observed Adam drily. 'He was enough to put you off us all for good.'

'Well, yes, that's true,' she admitted, 'but I don't think I'll have any more trouble from him, thanks to you.'

They walked on in silence for a while, their shoes making little sound on the soft path of leaf-mould and pine needles, then hesitantly Adam said, 'In actual fact, Natalie, I think we could have reason to be grateful to Lomax.'

'Grateful to him? But why? I don't understand.'

He sighed. 'It's difficult to explain, but I found myself being very over-protective towards you when he was around.'

'I noticed.' She gave a soft laugh.

'Well, eventually I was forced to examine why I was feeling that way, and I came to the conclusion that it was because I was jealous.'

'You, jealous? Of Roger Lomax?' Her eyes opened wide in amazement.

By this time they had reached the loch; Adam glanced at Natalie then, looking faintly embarrassed and as if to cover it, he let go of her hand, bent down and, picking up a flattish stone from the rocky shore, skimmed it across the water. They both watched as it bounced twice, three, four times before it disappeared beneath the smooth surface of the loch.

'The thing was, Natalie,' he continued as they walked on, 'I realised I was attracted to you, but I didn't want to admit it, even to myself, and for a while there I tried to pretend it wasn't happening. I'd made a bargain with myself, you see, a long time ago that I didn't want to get seriously involved again with anyone.'

She was silent as she recalled Jane's words, then Adam sighed again and said, 'I'm sorry, Natalie, I'm not sure that this is the time to be telling you all this, not when you're so worried about your father.'

Suddenly she stopped. Adam had walked on a few paces, but he turned to look at her, and she said, 'You do think he'll be all right, don't you, Adam?' There was a note of something close to despair in her voice.

He walked back and, putting his hands on her shoulders, he stared down at her. 'If his condition remains stable for another twenty-four hours I'd say he stands every chance,' he replied.

She gazed up at him, very aware of his nearness, his strength and his masculinity, which made her feel fragile and very feminine, and as he paused she said softly, 'But you were going to say that I'm as aware as you that anything can happen in a case like this.' She bit her lip and looked away. 'Of course I know that—haven't I said those selfsame words on so many occasions? But I had no idea, Adam, how incredibly difficult it is when the role is reversed. I

don't know what I'd do if he was to die.' Her voice
faltered and he instinctively tightened his grip on
her shoulders. 'After my mother died, Dad and I
became very close. . .' She trailed off helplessly.

'I remember your mother,' he said thoughtfully.
'She was a lovely lady; she was always so kind to me
when I came to visit with James—do you remember,
Natalie?'

'Oh, yes, I remember those visits only too well,'
she said.

'Why do you say it like that?' He frowned, and
when she lowered her head he put one hand beneath
her chin, lifting her face so that she was forced to
look into his eyes again.

She sighed, suddenly embarrassed. 'I'm not sure
that I should be telling you this, but I had what I
suppose was a schoolgirl crush on you,' she began,
'but you won't want to know about that now.'

She was aware that he had become very still, and
in the silence that followed the only sounds to be
heard were the gentle lapping of the waves at their
feet and the song of a lone blackbird in the pines
behind them.

Then slowly he said, 'On the contrary, I'd be very
interested to hear about it, because it was something
I knew nothing about.'

'You mean you never suspected? I thought James
might have told you—he teased me about it
enough.'

Adam shook his head, then, glancing around, he
took her hand and let her towards a large flat stone

at the edge of the loch. 'Let's sit here for a while. I want to know more about this.'

'There isn't really very much to tell.' Natalie laughed and, sitting down, she leaned back against a piece of rock that jutted out from the bank and, closing her eyes, lifted her face to the sun. It was warm there in the shelter of the rocks, with the belt of pines behind them protecting them from the chill of the March wind. 'I suppose you could call it hero-worship,' she said after a while. 'I used to keep calendars and cross off the days until your next visit. Then, if James arrived without you, I'd be devastated and shut myself in my room like some tragic Victorian heroine. But then when you did come you hardly noticed me, and when you did notice me you treated me like a little girl.' She fell silent then, her eyes still closed as she recalled those days of adolescent torment.

'I wish I'd known you felt like that,' he said softly, his gaze adoring every inch of her face.

'Why?' She opened her eyes. In spite of the intimacies they had shared earlier, when she saw the expression in his eyes she felt the colour flood her cheeks and she lowered her gaze in sudden confusion. 'What would you have done if you'd known?'

He gave a slight shrug.

'Don't forget, I was still a schoolgirl,' she added.

'What you're really saying is that I was far too old for you.'

'Too old for you to have been interested in me, even if you'd known how I felt.' As she spoke a

sudden noise made them both look up and a speedboat rounded the headland, the sound of its engine
shattering the peace. They watched in silence as it
streaked across the sparkling water in front of them
then disappeared from sight behind the belt of
pines.

'And how about now?' It was Adam who finally
broke the silence when the noise of the speedboat's
engine had become a mere hum in the distance.

'Now?' she murmured, hardly daring to raise her
eyes to his.

'Yes, do you still think I'm too old for you?'

'I don't think age differences matter at all
between adults and, besides, the difference doesn't
seem so much now.'

'So these feelings you had for me all those years
ago—what happened to them? Did they die or are
they just lying dormant, waiting to be aroused
again?'

Natalie was aware that her heart had suddenly
begun to beat very fast. She could hardly believe
what she was hearing, for in spite of what had
happened between them she had never really considered the possibility that Adam might have serious
feelings for her. 'I don't know, Adam,' she whispered at last. 'I suppose the question is, would you
want my feelings for you to be aroused?' She stared
into his dark eyes as she spoke and saw a spark of
amusement in their depths as he considered her
question.

'What if I said yes, that I'd very much like your feelings aroused—what then?'

She took a deep breath. 'I'd want to be sure that you meant it,' she answered. When he didn't immediately reply she added, 'Because, Adam, I'd have my doubts after what you said about not getting seriously involved again, and I don't want to get hurt.'

He lifted her hand and began to uncurl her fingers one by one from the tight little fist she had unconsciously created. 'Why would you have such doubts?' he asked at last.

'Because. . .because of Suzanne,' she said.

He lowered his head and there was a long silence, during which it seemed as if even the trees had stopped their whisperings and were motionless, waiting for his reply.

Natalie watched his features, the frown between the thick dark brows and the pain in the set of his mouth as he wrestled with some unseen demon.

'Ah, Suzanne,' he sighed, and it was so soft that she wondered if she had imagined it.

'From the moment you saw her you loved her so much, then you lost her,' said Natalie, then, shaken by how much pain it caused her to say it, she added, 'and I'm not sure you could ever again allow anyone to fill that place in your heart.'

Still Adam said nothing. He had lifted his head and was staring out across the loch to the distant mountains where smatterings of the winter snows still crowned the peaks, and just when Natalie had given up hope that he would deny her statement he said, 'When I met Suzanne I thought she was the most exquisite creature that had ever walked God's earth. I still thought so the day I married her. Everyone thought ours was the perfect marriage.' He turned his head then and looked at Natalie. 'They say some marriages are made in heaven, don't they? Well, Natalie, if that's the case, I can only say mine was made in hell.'

She stared at him in astonishment, unable to believe what she was hearing.

'I don't understand. . . I thought—we all thought that you and Suzanne. . .' She trailed off in bewilderment, uncertain how to continue.

'I know,' he replied bitterly. 'That was what you were meant to think, but it went wrong almost from day one.'

'But why?'

He was silent for a while and she allowed him the time he obviously needed to get his thoughts in some sort of order. Then at last he began to speak, and as the story of his marriage unfolded Natalie listened in stunned silence.

'I should never have married her,' he began. 'And as far as that goes I shall accept some of the blame. I should have got to know her better, but I didn't; I was so obsessed with her that it was only later that I realised we were totally incompatible. Our lifestyles were completely opposite; so were her interests and mine; even her friends and mine.' When Natalie remained silent he glanced at her and said, 'Oh, I know what you're thinking, that if we'd really loved each other those difficulties could have been overcome, some compromise could have been reached, and at first I too believed that, but as time went on I knew it was only me who was willing to reach any compromise, not Suzanne. But still I continued to give in, to grant her every whim, even though I now knew that my wife was totally self-centred. I know we should have discussed the question of children before we were married; I'd turned thirty and was keen to start a family, but Suzanne was dead against it. She feared pregnancy would ruin her figure and end her modelling career, and she certainly wasn't prepared to undertake the responsibilities of motherhood.'

'There are many women like that——' Natalie began uncertainly.

'I know,' he interrupted, 'and if those had been the only difficulties I think I could have overcome them.'

'You mean there were more?'

He nodded. 'I mentioned the fact that we had separate friends?' He threw her an apprehensive glance as if he found it almost impossible to continue. Then when Natalie nodded he carried on slowly, choosing his words with care. 'My friends were almost all in the medical world, which I suppose was understandable, and Suzanne's from the world she moved in—other models, agents, designers.'

'Also understandable,' said Natalie.

'I agree, and perfectly acceptable—or so I at first thought. I tried hard to adapt to their ways, but their values were very different from mine, and Suzanne and I had one row after another.'

'Their values?' Natalie frowned.

'Yes.' He hesitated. 'The main one being fidelity.'

She stared at him. 'You don't mean Suzanne. . .?'

'I mean especially Suzanne.' He gave a short bitter laugh. 'I don't think she'd even heard of the word.' He started to say more but stopped, as if he couldn't bring himself to tell her something, then, taking a deep breath, he said, 'Even on our honeymoon. . .'

'Your honeymoon?' Natalie was aghast as she recalled how ecstatic Suzanne had seemed to be at her wedding and how much in love with Adam they had all thought she was.

'Yes,' he replied bitterly. 'On the cruise she started a flirtation with one of the ship's officers. At first I thought it was innocent fun—or, rather, that was what I wanted to believe, but, deep down, even then I had an uneasy feeling. Eventually it became embarrassing, and I tackled her about it. She laughed at me and told me not to be such a bore. I decided to try and ignore it, but gradually I recognised her need to be constantly desired by the opposite sex. I persuaded myself it was harmless, but in the months that followed I quickly realised that was exactly what it wasn't.'

'But why did she marry you?' asked Natalie. 'She seemed to be so much in love with you.'

'She was in love with the idea of being in love. She wanted romance and glamour in her life, and, although she liked the concept of marriage, the reality was a different matter. She once told me she thought the image of a famous fashion model and a consultant surgeon was very romantic. When I pointed out that I was still only a registrar she simply laughed and told me to hurry up and get to the top of the tree, as she called it.'

'And now you have,' said Natalie quietly.

'Yes, ironic, isn't it?' He glanced at her, then, leaning forward, he plucked a blade of grass and began chewing the stem. 'She never knew that. I didn't get my consultancy until after her accident.'

Natalie looked at him curiously. 'You said once, Adam, something about unusual circumstances at the time of her death. What did you mean?'

He was staring out across the loch again to last year's brownish-purple heather on the hills and the mountains beyond, and at first Natalie thought he wasn't going to give her an answer. Then slowly he turned his head, and there was a look of such anguish in his eyes as he relived the past that it tore at her heart.

'In spite of what people assumed, we hadn't been together the night of her death,' he said simply. 'In fact, we hadn't been together for some days. Suzanne had been sleeping with some pop star. I knew about it, but I think by then I'd stopped caring what she did. She'd systematically been destroying my love for her with her constant affairs.' His voice caught, then he took a deep breath and continued, 'Anyway, after one particularly violent argument I told her to get out. A few days later, it seems, she'd left this guy's bed in the early hours of the morning and was on the motorway, travelling to a modelling assignment, when she crashed her car.' After a moment's silence he added, 'You know the rest.'

Natalie couldn't speak, but she reached out instinctively and touched his arm. He glanced down at her hand and swallowed hard.

She stayed silent long enough for him to get himself under control, then softly she said, 'Why didn't you tell anyone?'

'How could I?' he said simply. 'Particularly after what happened to her?'

'Couldn't you have brought yourself to tell me or James?'

Adam shook his head emphatically. 'Especially not you or James. She was your cousin, damn it, she was family. How could I blacken her memory for you all? And if I had, how could I have been sure you'd have understood, or even believed me? There was no hint of any scandal at the time—God knows how the Press never got hold of it, but they didn't. I suppose I should be thankful for small mercies and that at least she was discreet.'

'More likely she was afraid of jeopardising her career,' said Natalie grimly.

'You're getting the picture, then.'

'Yes, Adam, I think I am.'

'And do you believe me?' He caught urgently at her arm.

'Of course I do. What reason would you have for lying? Besides, you're forgetting something: you might not have wanted to tell me because Suzanne was my cousin, but equally, because she was my cousin, don't you think I didn't have some idea what she was like?' When he didn't answer she went on quietly, 'I didn't, of course, know about her promiscuity, but I did know she'd always been extremely selfish, and throughout her childhood she constantly craved admiration and always wanted it all her own way.'

Adam sighed. 'I still wouldn't have wanted to tell you. In fact, I'd vowed never to tell anyone the truth.'

'So why have you chosen to tell me now?'

He stared at her for a long moment. 'Because I'm in love with you,' he said simply at last, and Natalie felt her heart leap, but before she could say anything he continued, 'I never, ever thought it would happen again, and even though Suzanne had killed my love for her it didn't stop me grieving deeply for her and for what I'd once felt for her. I also had my guilt to contend with. Oh, yes,' he said when he saw Natalie's surprised expression, 'I suffered agonies of guilt after she died, wondering if I'd done all I could to make the marriage work. It was then that I vowed I'd never tell anyone what had really happened, but then I met you, and gradually I've realised that you had quite the wrong picture of my life with Suzanne.

Somehow you seemed to be under the impression that my love for her was totally irreplaceable, so I needed to set the record straight.'

As he'd been speaking he had turned and had drawn her into his arms, and was now holding her tightly against his chest as if he was frightened that she was a figment of his imagination and would disappear.

But for the moment Natalie was content to rest her head on his chest and savour the fact that he had just told her that he loved her. The impossible had actually happened, and the idol of her teenage dreams had admitted that he was in love with her, but, more important than that, the man he had become since, the man she had come to love in the past few weeks, had fallen in love with her.

For a moment she couldn't believe it, and she knew she would need some time to get used to the idea, then, as she thought how Adam had aroused her desires that night at Sheridan House and then of the exciting lovemaking they had shared earlier, she knew she wanted to believe it more than anything in the world.

'When did you know you loved me?' she whispered a little later as she gazed adoringly at his profile.

'I think from the very moment I saw you in church at James's wedding,' he replied.

'But how could you be sure? After all, you hardly knew me, and you've just admitted you fell for Suzanne in much the same way. How did you know it wasn't just a question of history repeating itself? I am, after all, Suzanne's cousin.'

'You're as different from Suzanne as it's possible to be—as I believe I once told you.'

Natalie pulled a face. 'You did, and I thought you meant that I could never match up to her.' She frowned. 'So, when you said you didn't want to get seriously involved, it wasn't because you thought you could never find anyone like Suzanne again?'

'Quite the opposite. After one disastrous marriage I didn't have any desire to repeat the exercise—that is, until I met you again. Even then, as I told you, for a while I fought my feelings, then, all the time I was in Brussels, I thought I'd lost you to that idiot Lomax. I couldn't wait to get back, then when I did I found you dancing with him at the club.'

'And I thought you were involved with the woman you brought back to Sheridan House that night,' said Natalie with a rueful smile.

'Good Lord, no,' he said. 'She was yet another partner who'd been lined up for me by one of my well-meaning friends. On that particular night I'd escorted her to an art exhibition which had been planned weeks before. But the night I first kissed you I knew you were the woman I wanted to spend the rest of my life with. I knew, however, that I had to tread carefully; I wasn't sure how you felt about Lomax, and you'd seemed so annoyed when I'd tried to warn you about him, but none of that stopped me feeling the way I did.'

As he spoke he stood up and drew Natalie to her feet, then before she had time to even think what was happening he cupped her face in his hands and brought his mouth down on hers, and for several blissful moments she gave herelf up to the sheer pleasure of being kissed by him. Her response was completely spontaneous and she sensed his delight as she allowed her arms to encircle his neck and her fingers to sink into his thick dark hair.

Between kisses he said, 'Dare I hope that there's a chance you might come to feel the same way?'

She laughed, pretending to consider, then said, 'Well, seeing that you love Scotland, that we're both members of the medical profession and that I've been madly in love with you for as long as I can remember, I'd say there's every chance.' Then, seeing his look of sheer pleasure, she lifted her face again to his.

While they had been talking the sun had sunk behind the mountains and a chill breeze was rippling the surface of the loch, and when they at last reluctantly drew apart Natalie shivered slightly, and Adam glanced at his watch.

'At this precise moment there's nothing I'd like better than to take you back to the hotel and make love to you all over again,' he murmured as he gazed down into her eyes. 'But if we're to get to the hospital we shall have to leave soon. So what I want to do will have to wait until later.'

With his arm around her, they left the little shelter in the rocks and retraced their steps up the path

from the loch beneath the pine trees and across the
smooth lawns to the hotel, and, although the March
wind did its best, Natalie was oblivious to its chill
and was only aware of a warm glow of contentment.